Marketing
UNDERCOVER BOSS
LEXY TIMMS

Marketing

Undercover Boss Series, Volume 1

Lexy Timms

Published by Dark Shadow Publishing, 2021.

MARKETING

First edition. March 31, 2021.

Written by Lexy Timms.

Also by Lexy Timms

A Bad Boy Bullied Romance
I Hate You
I Hate You A Little Bit
I Hate You A Little Bit More

A Burning Love Series
Spark of Passion
Flame of Desire
Blaze of Ecstasy

A Chance at Forever Series
Forever Perfect
Forever Desired
Forever Together

A Dark Mafia Romance Series
Taken By The Mob Boss

A Dating App Series
I've Been Matched
You've Been Matched
We've Been Matched

A "Kind of" Billionaire
Taking a Risk
Safety in Numbers
Pretend You're Mine

A Maybe Series
Maybe I Should
Maybe I Shouldn't
Maybe I Did

Assisting the Boss Series
Billion Reasons

Duke of Delegation
Late Night Meetings
Delegating Love
Suitors and Admirers

BBW Romance Series
Capturing Her Beauty
Pursuing Her Dreams
Tracing Her Curves

Beating the Biker Series
Making Her His
Making the Break
Making of Them

Betrayal at the Bay Series
Devil's Bay
Devil's Deceit
Devil's Duplicity (Coming Soon)

Billionaire Banker Series
Banking on Him
Price of Passion
Investing in Love
Knowing Your Worth
Treasured Forever
Banking on Christmas
Billionaire Banker Box Set Books #1-3

Billionaire CEO Brothers
Tempting the Player
Late Night Boardroom
Reviewing the Perfomance
Result of Passion
Directing the Next Move
Touching the Assets

Billionaire Holiday Romance Series
Driving Home for Christmas

Temporary CEO
Caught in the Act
Never Tell A Lie
Fake Christmas
Fake Billionaire Box Set #1-3

Firehouse Romance Series
Caught in Flames
Burning With Desire
Craving the Heat
Firehouse Romance Complete Collection

Forging Billions Series
Dirty Money
Petty Cash
Payment Required

For His Pleasure
Elizabeth
Georgia
Madison

Fortune Riders MC Series
Billionaire Biker
Billionaire Ransom
Billionaire Misery
Fortune Riders Box Set - Books #1-3

Fragile Series
Fragile Touch
Fragile Kiss
Fragile Love

Great Temptation Series
The Devil's Footsteps
Heaven's Command
Mortals Surrender

Hades' Spawn Motorcycle Club
One You Can't Forget

One That Got Away
One That Came Back
One You Never Leave
One Christmas Night
Hades' Spawn MC Complete Series

Hard Rocked Series
Rhyme
Harmony
Lyrics

Heart of Stone Series
The Protector
The Guardian
The Warrior

Heart of the Battle Series
Celtic Viking
Celtic Rune
Celtic Mann
Heart of the Battle Series Box Set

Heistdom Series
Master Thief
Goldmine
Diamond Heist
Smile For Me
Your Move
Green With Envy
Saving Money

Highlander Wolf Series
Pack Run
Pack Land
Pack Rules

Hollyweird Fae Series
Inception of Gold
Disruption of Magic

<u>Deceived</u>
<u>Provoked</u>
<u>Betrayed</u>

Model Mayhem Series
<u>Shameless</u>
<u>Modesty</u>
<u>Imperfection</u>

Moment in Time
<u>Highlander's Bride</u>
<u>Victorian Bride</u>
<u>Modern Day Bride</u>
<u>A Royal Bride</u>
<u>Forever the Bride</u>

Mountain Millionaire Series
<u>Close to the Ridge</u>
<u>Crossing the Bluff</u>
<u>Climbing the Mount</u>

My Best Friend's Sister
<u>Hometown Calling</u>
<u>A Perfect Moment</u>
<u>Thrown in Together</u>

My Darker Side Series
<u>Darkest Hour</u>
<u>Time to Stop</u>
<u>Against the Light</u>

Neverending Dream Series
<u>Neverending Dream - Part 1</u>
<u>Neverending Dream - Part 2</u>
<u>Neverending Dream - Part 3</u>
<u>Neverending Dream - Part 4</u>
<u>Neverending Dream - Part 5</u>

Outside the Octagon
<u>Submit</u>

<u>Pleasure</u>

Spelling Love Series
<u>The Author</u>
<u>The Book Boyfriend</u>
<u>The Words of Love</u>

Taboo Wedding Series
<u>He Loves Me Not</u>
<u>With This Ring</u>
<u>Happily Ever After</u>

Tattooist Series
<u>Confession of a Tattooist</u>
<u>Surrender of a Tattooist</u>
<u>Heart of a Tattooist</u>
<u>Hopes & Dreams of a Tattooist</u>

Tennessee Romance
<u>Whisky Lullaby</u>
<u>Whisky Melody</u>
<u>Whisky Harmony</u>

The Bad Boy Alpha Club
<u>Battle Lines - Part 1</u>
<u>Battle Lines</u>

The Brush Of Love Series
<u>Every Night</u>
<u>Every Day</u>
<u>Every Time</u>
<u>Every Way</u>
<u>Every Touch</u>
<u>The Brush of Love Series Box Set Books #1-3</u>

The Debt
<u>The Debt: Part 1 - Damn Horse</u>
<u>The Debt: Complete Collection</u>

The Fire Inside Series

Troubled Nate Thomas - Part 2
Troubled Nate Thomas - Part 3

Toxic Touch Series
Noxious
Lethal
Willful
Tainted
Craved

Undercover Boss Series
Marketing

Undercover Series
Perfect For Me
Perfect For You
Perfect For Us

Unknown Identity Series
Unknown
Unpublished
Unexposed
Unsure
Unwritten
Unknown Identity Box Set: Books #1-3

Unlucky Series
Unlucky in Love
UnWanted
UnLoved Forever

War Torn Letters Series
My Sweetheart
My Darling
My Beloved

Wet & Wild Series
Stormy Love
Savage Love
Secure Love

Marketing
UNDERCOVER BOSS
BOOK ONE

USA TODAY BESTSELLING AUTHOR
LEXY TIMMS

Copyright 2021 Lexy Timms

Undercover Boss Series

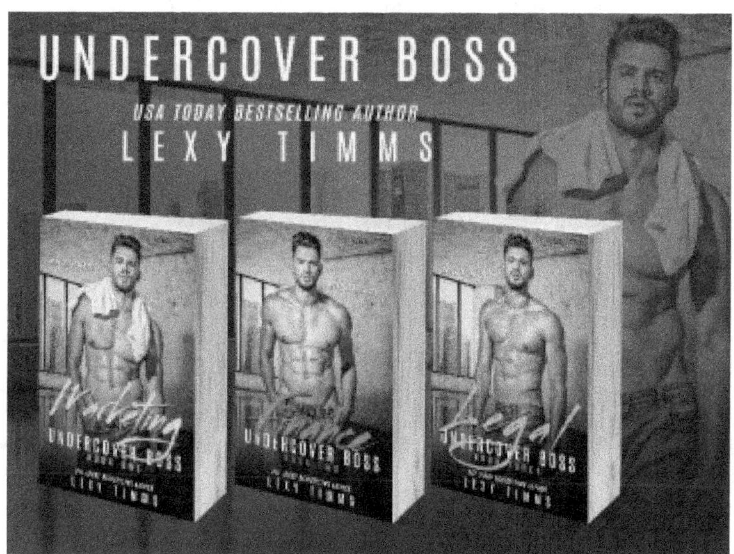

Book 1 – Marketing
Book 2 – Finance
Book 3 – Legal

Find Lexy Timms:

LEXY TIMMS NEWSLETTER:
http://eepurl.com/9i0vD
Lexy Timms Facebook Page:
https://www.facebook.com/SavingForever
Lexy Timms Website:
http://www.lexytimms.com

Want to read more...
For **FREE**?
Sign up for Lexy Timms' newsletter
And she'll send you
A paid read, for FREE!
Sign up for news and updates!
http://eepurl.com/9i0vD

Marketing Blurb

BE THE PLAYER, NOT the piece...

Adam Miller is just your average billionaire CEO of one of the largest tech and marketing companies in the country.

Katie Walters is just the PI he hires to figure out how one of his employees is stealing money from the company accounts.

But when they agree to go undercover together in one of his satellite offices, they're signing a contract neither of them fully understands. Their first meeting is electric, and before long, they're fighting a mutual attraction that they both know is a bad idea. When that attraction gets the better of them, they find themselves facing two problems:

1. You don't have sex with your boss—or the woman you've hired as your PI, and

2. Their attraction toward each other might just mean the thief ends up getting away.

Marketing
UNDERCOVER BOSS
BOOK ONE

USA TODAY BESTSELLING AUTHOR
LEXY TIMMS

Contents

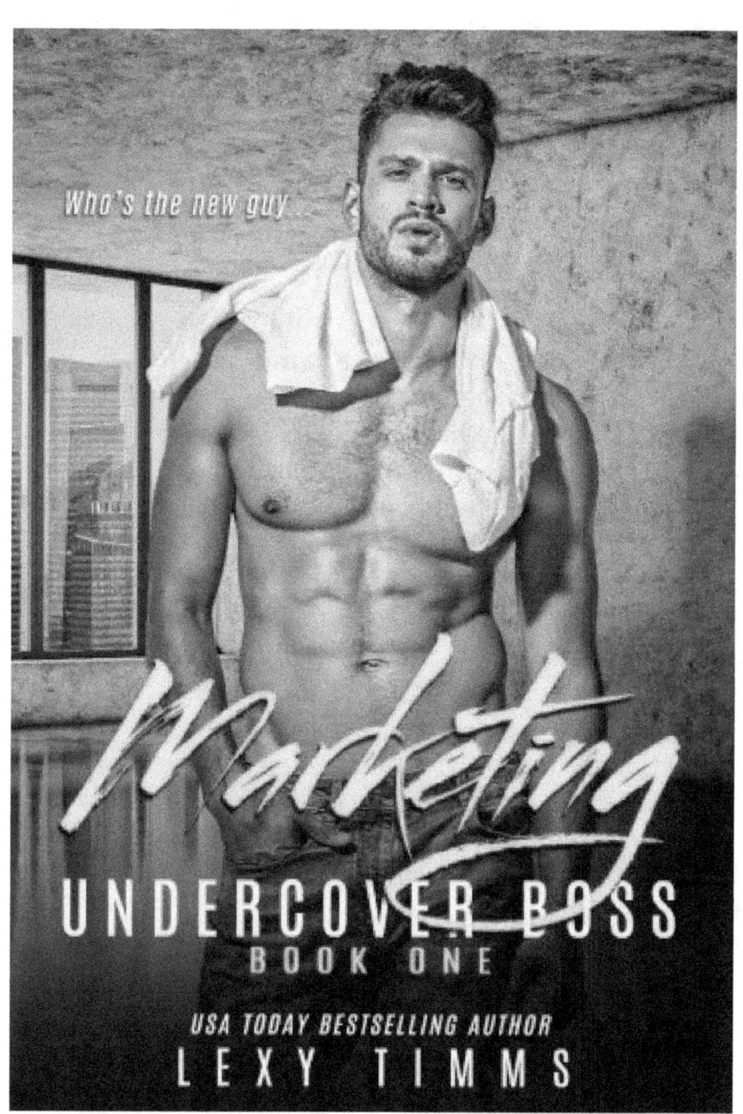

Who's the new guy...
Marketing
UNDERCOVER BOSS
BOOK ONE
USA TODAY BESTSELLING AUTHOR
LEXY TIMMS

CHAPTER 1

ADAM

"WHAT DO YOU MEAN, WE have $3 million just... missing?" I asked sharply, pressing the phone closer to my ear.

Surely I'd heard him wrong. Surely my accountant hadn't just said that we had $3 million in hard cash just... *missing*.

The pause on the other end of the line wasn't nearly as short as I'd hoped it would be—which I knew almost immediately meant bad news.

Look, when you're the head of a multi-billion-dollar company, you start to figure out how to read the room. How to take those pauses in difficult conversations, and what to read from them. Though if I was being honest, that right there was something I'd been good at right from the start. Long before I'd ever even imagined Miller and Co, the marketing and tech company that had grown from a tiny startup to something so big that we were now spread across five cities, I'd been good at reading people. I looked at their eyes, their mouths, what they did with their hands when they were saying something.

I watched their thoughts flit right over their faces.

And it had always given me a way to know what was coming. Sure, that hadn't been super useful when I was doing things like buying candy at the local corner store or even waiting for my race on the swim team, but it had always made me feel like I was one step ahead of everyone else.

Like I knew what to expect.

When I started Miller and Co, it had become something else entirely. A skill that had given me a leg up on the competition and told me exactly what my employees didn't want to say out loud.

Like right now, when Michael Ashman, my lead accountant, was keeping far too silent for far too long, after he'd just called me in my office to tell me, oh so casually, that he'd found a problem in the books. That he'd found a whole hell of a lot of cash just missing from the company accounts, and that he couldn't figure out where it had gone, or who had taken it, or even whether this was just some sort of clerical error.

"Michael," I said, trying to keep my voice calm. "What do you *mean* we have $3 million just missing?"

At first, my only answer was a sigh—which gave me even more reason to think bad news was coming. Then, evidently realizing that keeping quiet wasn't going to solve the problem, he finally started talking.

"I was doing a pretty standard quarterly audit of our books," he said quickly, his voice professional and completely emotionless. "You know, we do them every three months, just to keep an eye on things. And I came across a problem. Numbers weren't adding up. Or rather, they were, but not to the number they should be adding up to. The long and short of it, Adam, is that the company's bank account—the main account, the one that takes care of all our expenses—is $3 million short of where it should be. I don't have any more information for you than that."

I pulled my phone away from my ear and stared at it for a long, hard moment—like it was going to somehow change what Michael had just said.

Like it had turned into some sort of time travel device and would take me back to ten minutes ago, before Michael had told me, and rewrite history.

It didn't. Because newsflash: Phones are not actually time travel machines, and they can't change reality.

By the time I put said non-time-traveling device back to my ear, though, I'd allowed my brain to run with the problem, and had at least the start of an answer.

"We have records of every outgoing expenditure from the account?"

"Of course," he said, sounding like he was actually offended that I'd ask that.

I huffed out a laugh. I'd known Michael since I first started this company. He'd been my first hire, actually. And shocking him by pretending I didn't think he knew how to do his job had never gotten old.

"And I assume you've checked all of those to make sure they're valid."

Another affronted snort. "We're in the process of doing that now."

"Right," I said. "In that case, I don't suppose there's anything I can really do to help you. Keep me posted. And keep an eye on that account, would you? Make sure the discrepancy doesn't get any bigger than it already is."

"Absolutely," he said.

Then he hung up without saying goodbye. Which was also just like Michael. He was one of the most brilliant men I knew—which was why I'd hired him as my accountant—but the man was a whole lot better with numbers than he was with people.

I turned off my phone, put it down on my desk, and used my feet to push myself backward until I hit the window of my office. Then I turned my chair so I could see out ... and leaned forward to thunk my forehead against the glass.

Then I did it again.

And then again.

"Dammit," I breathed. Hearing that you were missing money was never a good thing. Yeah, the company was large enough that it wasn't going to interrupt any of our movements. We weren't going to have to turn off the electricity or anything like that. Weren't going to have to lay off employees or close one of the satellite offices or restrict our company's big Christmas party. At the end of the day, everything would be just fine.

But $3 million was still quite a bit of money. This was nothing to sniff at.

Suddenly, the intercom on my desk buzzed, indicating a call from my secretary.

I sat up, removing my forehead from the glass—leaving, no doubt, a mark that would give the cleaners fits—and spun back toward my desk.

"Adam?" Sonya, my secretary, asked, her voice taking on that weird tinny quality that intercoms give you. I had a momentary thrill that I had a secretary and that she called me on an intercom—two things that I didn't think would ever get old—and then I got down to business.

"Yep, I'm here. What's up? You're saving me from a truly horrendous meltdown."

"Glad to be of service. Oliver Brown just called and said he's on the way to the bar downstairs. He wants to know if you want to meet him there."

I was out of my chair so quickly that I actually forgot to answer her until I was at the door of my office, grabbing my coat and opening the door.

"Yes," I muttered to her as I strolled by her office, which sat just outside of mine. "Call him back and tell him yes, Sonya. I'll be out for the rest of the day."

Because if there was ever a time to get out of the office and go have a drink with my best friend and right-hand man, it was right now, when I'd just found out that someone was stealing from my company.

—◦—

OLIVER GAVE A LONG, low whistle, his eyebrows rising up so high I thought they might actually meet his hairline.

"Are you kidding me? Three million? That's not exactly chump change. How the hell did that happen, Adam?"

I gave him a look that said exactly what I thought of that question. "You're my CFO, Oliver," I pointed out. "Shouldn't I be asking you that question?"

Because yes, my best friend was also my CFO. And that meant that this little debacle fell under the umbrella of Things Oliver Should Have Handled Before They Got to Me.

He stared at me, open-mouthed, for several long moments before he broke into a grin.

"You obviously think I'm better at my job than I actually am," he finally said. "You don't actually think I'm in my office all day watching the numbers, do you?"

I grinned back, unable to stop myself. I'd known Oliver for most of my life, and I'd never been able to keep a straight face when he was making a joke. Even, it turned out, when that joke was about $3 million having gone missing from the company's ledgers.

"I'd have to be insane to think that you were actually doing your job," I agreed.

Oliver clinked his glass to mine, the grin growing. "Exactly. Besides, I thought my job description basically consisted of being available to save you from the office and get you down here to the bar at the drop of a hat. What else could you possibly need me for?"

Oliver was just fishing for compliments now. He knew as well as I did that he was a genius with numbers and sales, and had one of the sharpest minds in the building. Those were the reasons I'd hired him in the first place.

The fact that he could go downstairs with me to the bar was just a lucky benefit.

Still, that brilliant mind was why I was going to ask him what I was about to ask him.

"Actually, as long as you're offering..." I said quickly.

Oliver rolled his eyes and groaned. "Oh shit, what? I didn't mean for you to *actually* come up with something to need me for."

I laughed. "Nonetheless, you offered, and as such, I'm holding you to it. I need you to run the shop for me while I'm gone."

Now the smile dropped right off his face, replaced by a confused frown. "While you're gone? Where the hell are you going? I have to say, CEOs don't usually respond to finding out that someone is stealing from their company by getting up and going on vacation."

"Not a vacation," I told him. "A mission. I called Jack on the way down here. You know, the president over at Sterling. And he gave me some advice. Said he'd had something wonky going on in his company at one point, too, and had hired someone else to figure out where it was coming from. Some PI. Best in the game, evidently, and incredibly good with numbers and hacking. He said she solved his problem immediately, and I have to say, she's got the resume to prove it. She's collared some of the best white-collar criminals I've ever seen."

Oliver put a quick hand up. "Hold on, she? Are you telling me you've hired a woman PI to figure out what's wrong with our accounting?"

I grinned at the shock in his voice. Oliver was many things, but progressive had never been one of them.

"Yes, she. And not to figure out what's wrong with our accounting. With the rate she charges, I'd have to be insane to use her for something Michael can do in his sleep."

Oliver frowned. "What's she going to be doing, then? Teaching the rest of the office how to walk in heels?"

Dammit, there were times when he was actually annoying. How had I never noticed that before?

"Again with the rate she charges," I told him, fighting to keep from jumping around in my seat. "She's a PI. She's going to figure out who's doing what that's leaving the company account short."

"And I'm going to be...?" he asked.

"Running things here while I'm gone," I reminded him. "Nothing fancy. I just need you to make sure everyone else has someone to answer to. Make sure the kids don't throw any ragers while I'm out."

He tipped his head at me. "And where are you going to be again? While I'm supervising the teenagers, I mean."

I gave him a grin that felt both wicked and incredibly mischievous—two things that I hadn't expected to be feeling when I was up against something like someone possibly stealing money from my company.

What can I say? Being a CEO stuck in an office all day every day, dealing with numbers and marketing initiatives and employees, can get... monotonous.

Going out and doing what I was about to do sounded a whole lot more fun. Even if there was $3 million riding on it.

"I'm going undercover," I told him proudly. "Michael thinks the discrepancy in the accounting started with the Houston office. So I'm going down to Texas to see what I can find down there."

At this, Oliver actually sputtered with laughter. And since he'd just taken a sip of whiskey, that splutter resulted in whiskey spraying all over my face.

"Thanks very much," I said, wiping it off my cheek.

"Sorry," he said, completely unapologetically. "But you're going undercover? How? Why? When? And again, how?"

I picked up my own drink and tipped it, clinking my glass to his. "The PI is meeting me in Houston," I told him smugly. "And we're getting hired at the Houston office to infiltrate it. We're going undercover. Together."

CHAPTER 2

KATIE

THE MOMENT I LANDED in Houston, I was on my phone. And I mean literally the moment I landed.

The wheels had barely touched down before I was powering it back up, waiting the eternity it always took for the thing to turn on, and then thumbing right to my emails. We were in the middle of several very big cases, and I was waiting for some important files from my assistant.

"You're not supposed to turn that on until the plane has come to a stop, missy," the woman next to me muttered.

I glanced up, doing my best to paste a bright, cheery smile on my face. The woman, who looked like she was approaching ninety, had been lecturing me since we took off. My bag was taking up some of her space—even though it was shoved under the seat in front of us. I should have gotten an aisle seat if I was going to need to get up so often—even though I'd asked her if she wanted to switch to the window, and she'd told me no. I should have brought a tablet rather than my paperback, since it was kinder to the environment.

I shouldn't have worn flip-flops on the flight, since they left my toes unprotected.

Now the first couple of things I'd let blow over. I'd grinned and borne it when she said that I was getting on her nerves by getting up every so often to pace the aisle of the plane—something I had to do because I might go crazy, otherwise, being trapped in this cabin for so long. I'd just shrugged when she'd said that a tablet was better for reading and told her that I couldn't get over the feel of paper under my fingers or the smell of my favorite books.

I'd laughed when she told me that my glasses made me look like a librarian. I'd shaken my head when she asked whether I was planning to get married and settle down soon. I'd even blown it off when she asked me what I did and, when she found out I was a private investigator who worked on high-level white-collar crimes, told me that men didn't like women who worked too hard.

But telling me I shouldn't have worn flip-flops on the plane? That was where I drew the line.

How else were you supposed to get through security quickly and sit cross-legged in your seat?

I'd put my ear buds in, turned the music up nearly as high as it would go on my extremely old and beat-up iPod, and ignored her for the rest of the trip.

I shouldn't have been surprised, though, when she started going out of her way to annoy me again as soon as I took those earbuds out and powered up my phone.

"That thing will ruin the pilot's navigation," she hissed.

I gave her a stern look, trying very hard not to narrow my eyes at her. "In case you haven't noticed, we're now on the ground. So the nav system has pretty much already done its job. I think we'll be okay."

I didn't tell her that technically, I could have had my phone on when we were in the air, and we would have been fine. I didn't bother to go into details about how you could use this thing called airplane mode to turn off a phone's Wi-Fi and use it as just a device.

I didn't think she'd care to hear it, and honestly, I didn't want to have to talk to her any more than I already had.

I went back to my email, running through the things that had come in and looking for anything from Paisley, my assistant, about the cases we were working on right now. Particularly the one I was in Houston for.

The Miller and Co case. Nothing too complex, I didn't think. Honestly, it sounded more like they had an employee skimming off the top than anything else. But it was serious enough that the CEO had paid me a truly astounding amount of money to get my ass to Houston and investigate it personally.

It wasn't the sort of thing I normally did. But I'd taken one look at the amount he was offering me and said yes without thinking three times about the matter.

Now I was waiting for more information from said CEO, Adam Miller. The owner as well, it turned out. He'd been supposed to send Paisley more information right before I boarded the flight, and I wanted that in my hands so I could start processing it.

"What if you cause some sort of damage to the plane?" the woman beside me hissed.

Shit. I was going to have to start flying first class if this was what coach was becoming. Seriously.

"I think we'll be just fine," I said, glancing up at her one more time—and seeing that she was opening her mouth to argue with me. Because of course she was.

At that moment, though, the lead stewardess came over the intercom.

"Ladies and gentlemen, we've arrived at our destination," she said in that fake, cheery voice that stewardesses use when they're talking over the intercom. The one that they must really have to work themselves up to. "Please stay in your seats until the plane comes to a full and complete stop. You can power up all those electrical devices now, though. Get those messages I know you've been dying to check for the last three hours."

I gave the woman next to me a triumphant look, knowing that it was petty and not caring, and then went back to my email.

Nothing from Paisley, I noted. Dammit.

Still, I had the case files in my bag, and that would give me something to do tonight. I needed to get my story down so that tomorrow, when I got to the office where I'd be working for the next little while, I knew who I was supposed to be—and who this guy Adam Miller actually was.

———◉———

"YEAH, BUT DO YOU EVEN know who he is?" my best friend, Lindsey, asked through the phone. "I mean, you've googled him, right? You have seen him, right?"

"Of course I have," I lied.

True story: I hadn't. I'd left all of that up to Paisley, who had done all of the research on this guy and his company and sent me file after file after file. Which meant I knew all about this Adam Miller guy—like that he'd gone to Yale for college and then Dartmouth for his masters, and had come home to New York and immediately started his own marketing and tech company. And he'd done it so well that it had hit the big time two years later with an IPO that blew the rest of the offerings on that day out of the water. I knew he was single and didn't come from money, but had worked his fingers to

16

the bone to make that company what it was. I knew that he took a whole lot of pride in what they'd accomplished and that they were the leading marketing and tech combo firm out there. They had feet in both the marketing world and the tech world, and they regularly combined the two in ways that no one else had thought of.

I knew how much he was worth and how old he was and even that he didn't have any major health concerns.

And when Paisley had given me all of that, why would I have bothered to google him myself?

"Then you've seen what he looks like," Lindsey said. "Have you seen the picture of him on the beach? Holy. Freakin'. Hell. No, Hotter than hell, I bet."

Right, I hadn't seen what he looked like, and I definitely hadn't seen the picture of him on the beach, and I was pretty quickly realizing that I wasn't going to be able to fake my way through this one. Because Lindsey had always been able to tell when I was lying.

I grabbed my laptop, spun it around on the bed so it was facing me, brought up the web browser and quickly typed the name in, adding the company's name just for good measure.

The browser responded with fifty-two pages of images. Holy hell in a hand basket, was I glad I'd searched him before I met him in person.

The guy was drop-dead, melt-your-panties, make-your-mouth-water gorgeous. All danger and smolder and bright, glowing blue eyes, topped off by clean-cut chocolate hair and a jaw that looked like it could actually be used to cut glass. I ran my eyes quickly to the right, going over a couple of paparazzi pictures, and then found the beach picture Linds was talking about.

"Holy abs of steel," I muttered, knowing that she'd be able to guess by my statement—and the awe in my voice—that I definitely hadn't seen those pictures before. "What is this guy, some sort of supermodel-turned-entrepreneur?"

Lindsey's snort echoed through the phone. "Girl, I don't know what sort of supermodels you've been hanging out with, but that boy does not look like a model to me. He looks a whole lot more like the kind of guy you find parking his motorcycle in front of the club your mother told you never to go to."

I cocked an eyebrow. "And supermodels can't go to clubs or ride motorcycles?"

"Supermodels," she said aloofly, "don't walk around looking like sex on a stick. You live in New York. You know this as well as I do."

Okay, she was right on that one. Supermodels all looked like Clark Kent. The good boy. The hero.

This Adam Miller looked like the guy you dated when you were eighteen and didn't know how to spot danger when it was staring you right in the face with its rock-hard abs and chiseled jaw line.

I ducked in closer, staring at a picture, and finally enlarged it so I could see better.

Then I realized what I was doing and immediately pulled myself back down to earth. I canceled out of the web browser, shook off the chills those pictures had given me, and brought up the files Paisley had just sent me.

"Handsome or not, this guy has hired me for a job, and that's the reason I called you," I said, my tone all business. "I need your help coming up with a persona."

"A persona?" Lindsey asked, her voice on the edge of a giggle. "You've just googled Adam Miller and you want to talk about *work*? Are you actually serious right now?"

"Deadly serious," I said. "You know I don't usually go undercover to this degree. I want to make sure I'm ready. I need to figure out who I'm playing and learn everything about her, so I don't get caught off-guard by someone questioning me too closely."

"Katie," Lindsey said sadly. "There are times when I really think you're a fifty-year-old woman caught in a twenty-seven-year-old body. How the hell are you talking about going undercover right now? Look at that man!"

"I've seen him," I deadpanned. "And now I'm moving on. Are you going to help, or what?"

"Not if it means talking about a boring old case rather than that man," she said quickly. "Is it just me or does he have a chin dimple?"

I sighed. "It's just you."

She sighed as well. "That's it, where's my best friend and what have you done with her? The Katie Walters I know would be gossiping with me about this guy right now."

"The Katie Walters you know also wouldn't have a job if she was doing that," I noted quickly.

At that moment, there was a knock on the door of my hotel room. I jumped, because that's what you do when you're in a hotel by yourself and someone suddenly—and unexpectedly—knocks on the door.

I mean, you just never know when it could be a serial killer. Knocking on your door in a crowded hotel and just hoping you'll open it.

"Shit, Linds, I gotta go. Thanks for all the help," I said, coming down heavy on the sarcasm on the word 'help.' I hung up before she could answer me—or offer any other tidbits on Adam Miller and his abs.

I threw the phone on the bed, right next to my laptop, and hustled to the door, yanking it open before I thought about the fact that if there was a serial killer out there, I was now exposing myself to him.

Really smarter to use the peephole. To find out if the person on the other side of the door was wearing a 'Hello, I'm a Serial Killer' sign.

It wasn't a serial killer on the other side of the door, though. Unless Adam Miller had a secret identity after dark.

I stared at the man I'd just googled, my breath caught in my lungs and my stomach doing flips inside my body. Sheesh, I'd thought the man was good-looking in his pictures. But those pictures didn't hold a candle to what he looked like in real life.

First of all, he was taller than I'd expected. And broader. And sexier, his hair mussed and his jaw now sporting what looked like several weeks of beard growth.

"Adam?" I squeaked, my voice choosing that minute to stop working properly.

He shook himself and then gave me a quick grin. "In person. Katie, I presume."

And the moment he said that, I remembered that I was working for him. Hell, this man was my boss, for all intents and purposes—or at least a client.

And I was starting there ogling him like he was a fucking chocolate-covered strawberry.

I jerked my libido back into place, told it sternly to stay put, and stuck out a hand, all professionalism.

"In the flesh," I said with a polite smile. "I didn't know we had a meeting already. Did my assistant forget to tell me something?"

"Not at all," he said with a laugh. "Don't get her into trouble on my account. I knew I still owed you some files, and I thought I'd drop them off personally. You know, since we're in the same hotel and everything." He handed me a stack of papers, one eyebrow rising elegantly above the other. "Are you okay?"

I grabbed at the papers, already knowing that I was blushing. "I'm fine. I just wasn't expecting to meet you already. If I'd known, I would have put on something more professional."

I glanced down at my T-shirt and yoga pants. *Terrific, Katie*, I thought to myself. *Your first time meeting your new client, and this is what you're wearing.*

It was just so me. Biggest, richest client I'd ever had, and I was meeting him in the modern-day equivalent of sweats.

Classy.

He just laughed, though, and leaned in, his eyes going smoky and his voice dropping. "I work in pajama pants whenever I can. I promise I won't judge you for it." When he leaned back, leaving my heart racing, his laugh turned to a wicked grin. "I'll see you tomorrow at the office, Katie. Looking forward to working with you."

Then he was gone, and I was closing the door behind him and leaning up against it, my skin tingling and my stomach filled with butterflies. I felt heavy and light at the same time, full and empty, and generally like a tornado had come ripping right through my life without any warning. And I had one single thought on my mind.

If he could do that to me just by passing me a stack of papers, this was going to be a very long, very dangerous job. With a man that good-looking, and that charismatic? A man who could literally melt panties with a single look, and probably knew it and took advantage of it as often as he could?

Yeah, I was going to have to be extremely careful here. Extremely good and extremely disciplined. Because I had extremely strict policies about sleeping with clients. Hell, I had extremely strict policies about even thinking of clients as people I *could* sleep with. I didn't believe in messing around with the people I worked with, and as such, I didn't believe in noticing how hot they were or how their eyes raked up and down my body like they were cataloging every inch of it.

I had rules, dammit.

And I wasn't going to break those. No matter how much this guy was paying me.

21

CHAPTER 3

ADAM

THE NEXT MORNING, I arrived at the new office early.

Like half an hour early.

Don't look at me that way. I'd always been the kind of person who ran early, and it had never served me wrong. Seriously. It's so much better than getting to an engagement late.

Even better, it meant I was hanging out by the coffee cart when Katie Walters arrived. The lobby of the building was relatively big, but not so big that you could fit hundreds of people in there. This was, after all, one of our newest offices.

It hadn't gotten as big as the offices in New York or LA yet.

And that meant that when she walked in, all black pencil skirt and white blouse, black-rimmed glasses and red lipstick, I could see her quite clearly from the coffee cart in the corner.

Hot damn, the woman was gorgeous. I hadn't bothered to do much research on her before I hired her. Jack had recommended her, and that was good enough for me. I'd done a quick scan of her website, enough to see that her resume was impressive, and called her on the spot.

I mean yeah, she'd sounded sexy on the phone, but that didn't mean anything, did it?

It certainly didn't mean that a woman was going to wear a pencil skirt like it was a second skin and have eyes so light a green that they looked almost colorless, set off with curly brown hair that I wanted to run my fingers through. I wondered what she smelled like.

I'd been wondering that since I surprised her in her room last night.

And in that moment, as I watched her walk through the lobby, all high heels and complete business, I realized what I was doing.

Shit, I'd hired this woman to help me figure out whether this branch of the company was doing anything fuzzy with their numbers, and instead of treating her like a valued employee or someone who was probably three times as smart as me, all I could think about was the way she might smell and how she looked in a pencil skirt.

Fuck.

I straightened up, gave myself a very firm lecture about being a fucking professional rather than a playboy millionaire, like so many of my friends were, and settled my shoulders, putting back on my CEO mask.

I was here for a job. And I was a fucking adult. Not some fourteen-year-old boy who had never worked with a beautiful woman before.

I stuttered to a stop, though, remembering suddenly that I was here for a job—and not the CEO job that I generally went to work for. Instead, I was here as a salesman. Here to peddle the tech that my company built and sold to smaller companies.

I let the CEO swagger drop from my shoulders and looked around, wondering if anyone had been watching that little internal dialog—and the physical movements that had gone with it.

To my utter embarrassment, I met Katie's eyes from across the room and watched her tip her head and narrow her eyes at me, the corner of her mouth quirking.

Yep, she'd definitely caught me as I straightened into CEO mode... and then slouched back down into my salesman persona. And unless I was imagining it, she was laughing at me right now. Without laughing. And without acting like we knew each other, because we weren't supposed to.

Officially, for the story, we were here as people who'd only just met, and just happened to be staying in the same hotel.

And if this was going to work, we were going to have to stick to that story.

Which meant no inside jokes told from across the lobby of the Miller and Co building in Houston.

I tipped my head back at her and gave her a look of my own. *Are you looking at me? The guy you definitely don't know and certainly aren't working for right now?*

I watched the smile drop from her lips and her expression return to neutral, though she narrowed her eyes at me once. *I don't even know what you're talking about, Guy Who I've Never Laid Eyes on Before.*

She turned away with a shrug, and I did the same, heading for the elevators on the opposite side of the lobby.

And very carefully not examining the thrill that was still creeping across my skin at the wordless conversation we'd just had.

—————◈—————

JAMES ANDREWS, THE man who was going to be my boss while I was in this building, glanced through my resume one more time, then looked up at me with a condescending grin.

"Have to say, corporate doesn't usually send us new employees," he said, giving me the idea that he wasn't really a fan of the experience, but also wasn't going to say anything to anyone about it, since it would probably get him fired. "Still, I'm going to trust them to send us someone good. Why else would they bother, eh?"

He laughed, his cop mustache twitching with it, and I smiled back, liking the guy. Sure, he looked like he belonged in a '70s porno with that curly hair and mustache, but he also seemed really friendly. And like I said, I was good at reading people.

This guy seemed like a straight shooter. And I liked that. I liked knowing that good people worked for my company.

Then he narrowed his eyes at me and frowned, and I stopped liking him so much.

"You sure do look familiar," he said slowly. "I haven't met you before, have I?"

Shit. I'd done everything I could do when it came to a disguise. Grown out plenty of scruff. Donned heavy-rimmed glasses. Allowed my hair to grow out as much as possible.

Beyond that, I was just counting on the people in this office to be sort of oblivious. I mean, how often were they really looking at pictures of the CEO of the company? Surely they wouldn't recognize me. They didn't have any reason to.

But it occurred to me now—belatedly—that the head of the sales department just might. He'd probably seen my picture when they hired him, and he might even have been at some sort of welcome shindig back in New York.

I couldn't have him blowing my cover, though, as it would mean whoever was stealing money in this branch would get off the hook.

"You wouldn't believe how often I get that," I said quickly. "I guess I just have one of those faces."

His expression immediately cleared, and he nodded. "I get it. My best friend is the same. He looks like everyone and no one. It's impossible to take him anywhere without people claiming to recognize him. He says it's because he looks like Brad Pitt, but that's definitely not true."

We both laughed at that, and the knot in my stomach started to ease up a little bit.

I was just going to have to hope that no one else had been staring at the pictures of the corporate office. Because I wasn't leaving here—or dropping my disguise—until I knew what was going on in this office, and why it had cost me $3million.

⸺●⸺

WE MET IN THE BAR DIRECTLY after work by accident.

At least, that was what anyone who was watching us would have thought. I hoped. It was also, I supposed, what Katie thought, as we hadn't planned any of it ahead of time. But when I strolled through the lobby on the way to the pool area, desperately in need of some time in the hot tub—which this hotel had, as I'd checked specifically for that—and saw her in the bar, I'd had the best idea ever.

We weren't supposed to be talking, because we weren't actually even supposed to know each other. That was our story, and we had to stick to it if we were going to pull this whole thing off—which I needed for us to do.

But no one could be suspicious of two people who were staying in the same hotel happening to meet up in the bar of said hotel after their stressful first day at work, right?

Right.

I sauntered in, trying to look as casual as possible, and made right for where she was sitting at the bar, something that looked green and fruity on the surface in front of her.

"Of all the gin joints in all the world, you happen to be in the one that I happen to be walking by," I said, keeping my voice low and smooth. "Imagine meeting you here."

She jerked like she'd been deep in thought, slid the papers I now saw she'd been looking at to the side, and whirled toward me, her eyes big behind her glasses and her mouth caught in an O of surprise. When she saw me, of course, her entire expression changed.

Instead of surprised, she turned crafty, her eyes sliding to the right—into the room of the bar—and scanning the area quickly for anyone who might see us together.

"Don't worry," I told her, lowering my voice even more. "I checked out the entire place. No one from work is here."

She just snorted and turned back to me. Then her eyes went to the towel tossed over my shoulder and my T-shirt-clad chest.

I stood up a bit straighter, practically daring her to look. Because I knew what she was seeing: a well-muscled guy who filled out his T-shirt with no problem.

I'd worked hard on this body. Or rather... this body had been the gift I received for spending so much time in the gym, taking my daily work stresses out in a more physical manner. I'd never heard any complaints, and the corner of my mouth turned up in what I knew had to look like an extremely cocky smile.

Instead of returning it, though, she gave me the most deadpan look ever. "Is that how you always dress when you're out and about? Board shorts in case you happen to fall into a fountain or something? The towel to dry off afterward?"

Ouch. I actually cringed back a bit, surprised by her dry tone and the fact that she wasn't even *trying* to flirt.

"Well, no, but it is how I dress when I'm on my way to the hot tub," I said, giving her the grin that I knew from experience charmed the panties right off most women. "Mind if I join you?"

Her own mouth gave me a shade of a grin now, and I relaxed a little bit. "You sure you can take the time away from your date with the hot tub?"

I slid onto the barstool next to her. "Positive. Hot tubs are better when it's dark out, anyhow."

She tipped her head back and forth like she was considering it. "Is that in the rule book somewhere, or just a personal preference?"

"Both," I told her firmly. "What are you drinking?"

She paused for a full second before she said, "Madori sour. The perfect blend of sweet and sour out there."

I stared at the fluorescent green drink, trying to keep my face neutral. "It sure is... green."

"That's the best part," she said, picking the drink up and taking a long, slow sip in demonstration. "The lovely shade."

Then, to my complete surprise, she stuck her tongue out at me—and demonstrated that it was bright green, as well. The same color as the drink.

I laughed, shocked at this action from a woman who evidently dressed like a librarian and had a reputation for being better with numbers than anyone else in the business.

"How many drinks do you have to have to do that?" I asked. "Or is it like a green popsicle: two licks and you have the tongue of an alien?"

She gave me another serious look. "Are you saying all aliens have green tongues? Because I'm betting there are some bright red aliens out there who would love to prove you wrong." Then, surprising me even more, she pushed the drink in my direction. "As for how many it takes to change the color of your tongue, I guess you'll have to find out for yourself."

I paused, looking at the bright drink with something very close to distaste.

"Go on," she encouraged, a smile creeping into her voice. "I dare you. I double dog dare you."

I sighed. "You had to go all in, eh? How could I ever say no to a double dog dare?"

I picked the glass up, gave a huge internal groan at what I imagined I was about to experience, and took a quick sip.

I was shocked to discover that it was... good. Sweet and sour, as she'd said, with a combination of...

"Is that melon?" I asked, wrinkling my nose.

She took her glass back and took another sip, nodding. "Madori is melon-flavored, yeah. Combined with a shot of vodka and lemon and lime juice. Plus soda, if you're extra." She put the glass down and grinned at me. "And the best part is, it doesn't get you drunk. Which means I still have my entire brain ready and waiting for our first numbers discussion. Do you have some time?"

My brain jerked to a halt, rearranged itself, and then started going in a completely different direction.

Because I'd been doing Flirty with Cocktails Adam. And now it turned out we were doing Numbers and Work. Not exactly what I'd had in mind, when I was sitting at a bar flirting with a very pretty girl.

Though it was exactly what I'd hired her for. And she was my employee, officially speaking.

I was really going to have to keep that part in mind. She evidently was—which was both a blessing and a disappointment.

I told the bulge in my pants and the flutter in my general stomach area to go the hell away, and got down to business.

"Right. Numbers. You get anything good today? Any initial, first-day observations I should know about?"

Everything in the sales department had looked completely aboveboard to me. But we'd put Katie into the accounting department—partially so she could take advantage of her genius with numbers, and partially so she could keep an eye on the actual accounts. From there, we hoped, she'd be able to watch what everyone was doing, courtesy of the accounting software that literally tracked every employee's company expenditures.

If someone in that office was padding their accounts, that was where it was going to show up.

I hoped.

She shrugged. "Nothing that seems obvious. Though I did find a bunch of reporting errors from one of the higher-ups."

Her eyes went right to mine, and I knew she was thinking exactly what I was thinking. Reporting errors happened. But not in bunches.

And if Katie had found that in just one day, what else was she going to find in those accounts?

CHAPTER 4

KATIE

THE NEXT MORNING, AFTER sleeping far too hard in a bed that was entirely too comfortable—thank you, company account that was paying for a hotel I never would have booked on my own—I was up early and going through my case files on my laptop.

I was also talking to Lindsey about the case.

Wait, scratch that. It was a whole lot more like I was talking about the case and she was talking about Adam.

"Have you done anything with him yet?" she asked breathlessly.

"Like what? Traded recipes? Painted each other's toes? Stayed up all night sharing secrets about how we keep our companies running smoothly? No to all of the above," I told her drily.

She huffed out a sigh. "You know exactly what I mean, Katie. Don't pretend you don't."

"And the answer is that of course I haven't done anything with him," I told her, my voice still toneless. "He's a client, not a date."

"A client who *could* be a date," she replied coyly.

"Yes, because that's exactly what I need. A client who becomes a date who becomes something more and then suddenly becomes nothing at all, but manages to tell everyone what we did together when we were something more," I pointed out. "It would kill my reputation, and that would kill my company. Then again, I guess you don't have to think about these things, do you?"

Lindsey was a 1st grade teacher—though you wouldn't think it to listen to her talk—so she didn't have to worry about things like making sure her company was still running at the end of the day, and worrying about its professional reputation.

"Actually," I added. "Hold that thought. What you're asking me to do is essentially the same as if you slept with your principal, expected not to get caught, and expected everything to be okay even if you *did* get caught. I know you well enough to know you would never do that."

"Eeeeeeew, Katie, don't even say that," she groaned. "Take it back immediately. You've seen my principal. I don't want that picture in my head."

I remembered now that I did know who her principal was: a balding, pudgy old man, about seventy years old.

Lindsey might be a 1st grade teacher and wear appropriately teacherly dresses during the day, but at night she was a flirting machine, complete with the skintight dresses and dangerously high heels. I'd gone out with her a couple of times, realized that I did not have what it took to keep up with her, and restricted our girl nights to movies and popcorn from then on.

That hadn't stopped her from dragging our other friends out to the bars on the weekly. She was a connoisseur of wine and hot men, and she took her hobbies extremely seriously.

She would never in one million years have been caught making eyes at her principal.

"Okay, I take the picture back, but not the point," I told her quickly. "And the point is, I can't get messed up with him like that. Sure he's hot. Sure he could probably melt panties and unhook bras just by looking at a girl the right way. And he's richer than Midas. And has wicked eyes and a chin dimple. But none of that means anything. I'm here to do a job, and I'm going to get it done and then go home. With my panties unmelted."

She snorted. "For someone who doesn't want to have her panties melted, you're sure spending an awful lot of time cataloging his qualities."

"I had to catalog them to get them out of the way," I told her primly. "Now I have ideas I need to brainstorm for this job. Are you going to help me or what?"

"Can I actually choose 'or what'?" she whined. Then, after a short pause—where I did not say she could choose that option—she relented. "Fine, what do you need to talk about?"

I told her about the first day, and how I'd been assigned to the accounting department. We'd planned that, Adam and I, when we first came up with this plan. He was in sales and I was in accounting, because salespeople spent the most money and had access to the accounts, and the accountants had the easiest route to track anyone using those accounts. These were the most logical places to be, and

Adam had asked his HR department in New York to set it up so that we'd have easy entrees to the departments.

"Wow, you two sound like a spy couple from a movie," Linds said, her voice dreamy. "You're, like, running a mission together. Making a plan. Pretty soon you'll be sneaking into the office in the middle of the night, you in a black leather catsuit and him in a tux. You'll have to avoid the laser security system and it'll mean—"

"You have definitely been watching too many movies," I said, interrupting her. "I know exactly which movie you're picturing right now, and I can tell you that we are not doing anything like that. The only sneaking I'm going to be doing is through the computers, to pick up on who isn't declaring all the money they're spending—and who's directing money into their own accounts rather than to the vendors they're supposed to be buying from."

I could practically hear her pouting through the phone, and I almost laughed—until I glanced at the clock and realized what time it was.

"Oh shit, I'm late!" I shouted into the phone. "Shit! Shit! Shit! I thought I had more time. Dammit! I don't, and now I'm going to be late on my second day of work!"

I was already up and rushing around the suite, quickly gathering the things I'd need to get to the office. My laptop and backpack. My purse. My shoes.

Shit. Where the hell were my shoes?

"What the hell? My shoes, my shoes!" I nearly screeched.

"Woman, get a hold of yourself!" Lindsey screeched back. "Also, get off the phone. If you're late, you need to focus on that. And I don't need to hear the play-by-play."

I didn't even respond to her. I just hit End, threw my phone onto the bed, where it landed right next to my purse, and commenced the search for my other shoe, while trying to remember whether I had a ride share app on the phone I'd just thrown on the bed.

Then, as I was going to my knees to look under the bed for the offending shoe, I realized that it was going to be a whole lot faster to just grab one of the cabs downstairs. Because I was not going to be late for my second day at work. Even if the job was one big con in the first place.

⸻⸻◉⸻⸻

I WASN'T LATE TO WORK.

But I did get shuffled right into a training session, where the supervisor 'taught' me a load of things that I already knew like the back of my hand.

Luckily, sitting there being told to learn something you already know gives you a whole lot of time to let your brain move on to other, more important, things, and that was exactly what I did, giving my mind free rein when it came to the case itself and where—and how—I wanted to look for discrepancies in this office.

By the time we got out of the training session, I had a mental list of places to look and another list of specific people I wanted to look for. I'd come down here with ideas already, of course, but now that I was actually here and seeing everything in person, certain things were becoming more clear to me. This office, despite what I was sure had been very good guidance from corporate in New York, had really horrible record-keeping. Most of the employees, from the assistants on up to the top salespeople, had accounts of their own, which they could use to order pretty much anything they wanted. And though that wasn't against company policy, the fact that they could do it without any approval from their superiors—or any need to go through an audit once a month or so—meant that there were plenty of ways for people to be taking advantage.

I found it shocking that someone had been able to take advantage to the tune of $3 million, but given the holes in their processes, I wasn't eliminating the possibility that multiple people were doing this and just hadn't been caught.

That was the list of people I wanted to look at. I'd found some big discrepancies under a single supervisor, and I was thinking that his department was a good place to start looking.

Even if I didn't find the person we were searching for, I'd help the company itself plug up some holes. And there was nothing wrong with that.

"Okay, guys," my supervisor said suddenly. "As a reward for a great month of work, we're taking you out to lunch. Sales is going to be joining us. Leave whatever you're doing, and let's get the hell out of this joint!"

I tipped my head, surprised. We were being taken out to lunch? Along with sales?

That seemed extravagant. It also meant that I was about to go out to lunch—on company time—with Adam Miller.

The idea made my stomach do a ludicrous somersault move, and then come flopping back down.

I told it very sternly to be still, reminded my entire body that we were doing this the professional way, and set out for my supervisor's desk, my professional face on and a promise not to even look twice at Adam while we were at lunch fresh in my brain.

⸻ ◉ ⸻

OF COURSE, THAT WHOLE 'don't even look twice at Adam' thing worked really well until he actually came and sat right next to me, his tray full of what looked like everything this buffet had to offer.

I glanced at the tray and smiled, despite myself. "What, you're worried they're going to run out of food between now and when you might go back for seconds?"

"Honestly, I'm sort of regretting that they don't have a bar," he replied, sounding completely serious. "Because I'm thinking a Madori sour would be the perfect complement for this meal."

"Even if it turns your tongue green?" I asked. Despite myself.

Because I knew I shouldn't. I knew I should be talking to him about the case. But I couldn't seem to help myself.

"Even if," he said firmly. "Though I still don't believe that it was actually the drink that did that. I think you had a green apple Jolly Rancher hidden in your purse."

"The better to fool you with," I agreed, also serious, and bumped him with my shoulder.

"You two know each other already? That's terrific! Look at you, making friends when you've only been here two days. That's what I love about this company. It's got such great culture."

Adam and I both froze, our shoulders way too close and the smiles still on our faces, and sat stock still as a middle-aged woman came walking around the table. I didn't recognize her—and I was sure I would have, what with her bright orange hair and blue eyeshadow, which I was willing to bet was a personal style choice she made every single day. Adam evidently did, though, because I felt him relax slightly.

33

"Evelyn, have a seat," he said warmly. "Katie, this is Evelyn. She works in sales with me. Well... she works in the same department. I can't exactly say that she works with me, can I?"

He forced a laugh, but I watched the woman's eyes run up and down his body, her face considering, and realized he'd already wrapped this woman around his little finger.

Clever boy.

"It's nice to meet you," I said, forcing my voice into that warm space I used with people I also needed to charm. "We don't actually know each other that well, but the company has put us both up in the same hotel until we find places of our own, so we've seen each other in the lobby."

"The curse of the new kids is to be grouped together so much they become friends," Adam continued, nodding. "If Katie's not careful, I'll be making her eat lunch with me every day, just so I have some company."

Evelyn actually giggled. "She'd be a lucky girl, I have to say. I don't think she'd complain about it."

I laughed along with her, agreeing that it wouldn't be the worst thing.

But on the inside, I was screaming at myself. Adam and I couldn't afford for our cover to be blown. Not if we were going to accomplish our goals. And yet I'd been sitting here flirting with him like a complete rookie.

I needed to keep my eye on the prize. Not fall for his charm act like this was my first carousel.

And from now on, that was exactly what I was going to do. Not fall for his charm, I mean.

From now on, I was going to act like this was nothing more than a job with any other client. And I was going to mean it.

CHAPTER 5

ADAM

AFTER OUR LUNCH NON-date—and the excuse we'd managed to work together to make up on the fly, which I'd thought was pretty good, considering—I didn't see Katie again for several days.

It wasn't for lack of trying.

I mean, not trying, per se. I couldn't exactly go to her floor in the building and ask after her, and if I didn't see her in the foyer of either the building or the hotel, then I was pretty much shit out of luck. I mean, I knew what room she was in at the hotel, but we'd also come really close to being discovered already, and I knew without having to ask her that neither of us was willing to walk that particular line any closer to the edge than we had to.

We were here to do a job, and though I assumed it was slightly more important to me than it was to her, it was also her reputation on the line. Get fingered and our time here would be over—as would the investigation. Because if anyone found out who we were, I knew it would spread through the building—and then the company—like wildfire.

Whoever was stealing from me would hear about it, and they'd run. I'd never recover the money they'd stolen from me.

I'd never be able to make sure they were prosecuted for having done it.

And—and this might have been the biggest factor in my mind—Katie and I would be going our separate ways, never to meet again.

Sure, okay, that sounds all melodramatic, but it was the truth. I'd started looking forward to our little accidental meetings. I'd been looking for her specifically, and her pencil skirts and glasses, when I walked through any room.

I'd started craving that little jolt it gave me when I saw her.

All of which led to me creeping toward her room at 9 at night later that week, my eyes on the people around me and, I was sure, looking the opposite of subtle.

Have you ever noticed how someone who is sneaking manages to make it completely obvious that they're doing so? Like the very act of trying to be sneaky makes them incredibly obvious?

Yeah, I was pretty sure that was me as I entered the elevator on my floor and hit the button for 9. I'd known where she was since that first night, of course. But I hadn't come down here since that first night, when I dropped off paperwork to her.

I'd been way too paranoid about making it obvious that we actually knew each other.

Tonight, though, I'd come with a plan. And props. I had an entire binder under my arm, and though it was fully of blank pages, if anyone asked, I'd tell them I was working on making sure my own accounts were under control, and since I happened to know that someone from the finance department was actually in this hotel, and since I further knew her from having shared a cab to the office a time or two, I just figured I'd take advantage of it and check in with her.

The excuse wouldn't hold up if anyone asked to see the binder. But I couldn't see why anyone from our office would be in this hotel to start with. Or why they'd actually ask to see the binder that supposedly held the records of my accounts from work.

If they were and they did, I'd just have to make something else up on the fly.

Seconds later, the elevator dinged to let me know that I was on the 9th floor, and I got off the elevator and looked to the right and the left—like someone who's being sneaky and doesn't want anyone else to notice what they're doing.

I huffed a breathy laugh at myself, told myself to calm the hell down and just get it done, and turned right off the elevator bank, toward her room.

The moment I took that first step, I realized that there were probably several problems with my plan aside from the possibility of getting caught. Katie might be asleep, for one. She might not want to see me, for two.

Or she might have someone else in that room with her.

I didn't even know where that last thought came from, or why it should matter to me. It wasn't like I was dating her, after all. We were just coworkers. Kind of. A client and his personal investigator.

Who happened to be a completely beautiful women that would have caught my eye even in the most crowded of crowded rooms, and who was also quite possibly the smartest person I'd ever met.

Not that any of that mattered. We had a job to do and we were doing it, and that was all there was to it. Who cared if she had the most perfect face known to man, with hair that I wanted to thread my fingers through and a waist that I wanted to wrap my hands around? Who cared if her skin was the softest ivory and her eyes were such a light green that—

"My goodness, Adam, get a grip," I muttered, forcing my brain to give it up.

She was just my PI. I didn't have a thing for her, and I didn't care if she had anyone else in that room with her. I just wanted to check in and see how things were going. That was it. That was all.

When she opened the door to her room in her pajamas, though, and my eyes flitted past her to see that the room was empty, I immediately felt a whole lot better than I had any right to feel about such a thing.

"Adam," she said, frowning. "Is something wrong? What are you doing here?" Then her eyes widened and she glanced to the right and the left.

Without any hesitation whatsoever, she reached out, grabbed my arm, and yanked me into her suite.

"What are you doing here?" she hissed again. "We can't be seen together. You know that."

"Well—" I said, my eyes roving around her room.

She had clothes thrown all over the place, as well as several stacks of books on various surfaces. The bathroom had her robe thrown over the door and towels on the floor.

There were shoes *everywhere*.

I turned back to her, somewhat surprised at the state of the room. I'd thought she was a perfectionist librarian type. Honestly, the fact that she did things like stack books on every table available and carpet the room in shoes...

Damn, it made her even sexier. It shouldn't have. But it definitely did.

I yanked my thoughts back to the question that she'd asked me, knowing already that going down that road was nothing but trouble.

"Everyone knows we're staying in the same hotel," I told her. "No one is going to think twice about seeing both of us here. Besides, I already thought of a story."

She put a hand on her hip. "A story? Really? Is it better than us being forced together because we're the new kids in the office?"

"Hey, that totally worked," I said defensively. "And it is, actually." I held up the binder I'd brought with me. "I know you work in finance, and I wanted to make sure that my accounts were in order before I turned them in to my boss. Since you're in the same hotel and everything..."

I gave her a slow, suggestive wink, and suppressed the proud smile I could feel coming to my lips.

Her own lips quirked in response.

"Okay, that's clever," she admitted. "But what's really in that binder? Because I know you can't have that many accounts to audit. You haven't even been in that department for a week."

I held the binder flat and flipped it open to display a page inside.

"Nothing," I said simply. "But it was the best excuse I could think of for coming to your room, and I knew I'd need a prop if anyone questioned me about it."

She looked down at the blank page, her eyes going narrow, and then glanced back up at me. "So why are you really here? Since you obviously don't actually need help with your accounts."

I walked over, put my binder on the desk, and pulled up a seat, sitting down and folding my hands on the desk. "I figured it was time we had a business meeting. Where are we with this case, and where are we going to go from here?"

At my question, her entire face lit up with excitement. She rushed over to her briefcase and pulled out a stack of papers, then sat herself across the desk from me, spreading them all out in front of her.

I noticed that all of her papers had writing on them. Every. Single. One.

"That's... quite a few notes," I noted vaguely.

She looked up and gave me a proud grin that echoed the one I'd been fighting off earlier. "I know. I've had a lot of thoughts while I was in the office, and the best thing for me is to get them all down on paper before they fly right out of my head."

No wonder Jack had recommended her, I realized. She evidently kept her shoes anywhere *but* the closet, but was almost terrifyingly organized when it came to the cases she was working.

Before I could ask her if she'd found anything out, though, there was a knock at the door.

"Room service!" the person on the other side called out.

Katie looked from the door to me, both her eyebrows lifted up to mid-forehead. "I didn't order anything. Did you?"

"Of course," I said, getting up and walking toward the door. "I need your brain firing on all cylinders while we have a chance, and I figured food would help us both think."

I opened the door to room service and looked over the trays of food they'd brought, feeling... well, proud.

Katie, who had appeared behind me, was looking as well.

"What did you do, order everyone on the menu?" she asked quietly.

I nodded. "Pretty much. I didn't know what you would want. Or how long we'd be here."

"Presumably only for a couple of hours, max," she said, backing up so the waiter could wheel the trays in. "I don't think we'll get through even half of that."

I plucked a strawberry off the cart as the waiter wheeled it by. "You'd be surprised at how much I can eat," I said, grinning at her.

⸻⸻◉⸻⸻

AN HOUR LATER, WE'D been through all of Katie's notes and had built several new documents on her laptop. I knew that the guy she'd found with the incorrect numbers was someone who was relatively high up in the sales department, though I didn't recognize his name, and that he had lots and lots of numbers that seemed 'wrong,' according to Katie.

So far, he was our only lead. Though Katie was also investigating the people who worked for him, as he could be covering for them.

"We just don't know," she said, picking a croissant apart as she stared at her notes. "Has it occurred to you that this could be the work of more than one person?"

I put the remains of my sandwich down, thinking. Because no, it hadn't.

"Do you think it is?" I asked quietly.

She just shrugged. "That's what I'm here to find out. I'm going to be at my desk without anyone else tomorrow, and the first thing I'm doing is breaking into this Charles Ray's accounts. I want to see what he does when no one else is watching. I want to see what he might be hiding."

Right, okay, normally I would have said that was a really big violation of the guy's privacy, and that HR was going to have a field day with her.

But I'd basically hired her to do just that. And I wasn't going to stop her.

"How did you decide to be a PI, anyhow?" I asked. "This doesn't seem like it would be what a little girl dreamt of for her future."

She looked at me for a moment like she was wondering whether I actually wanted the truth or not. Whatever she saw, though, must have convinced her, because she nodded and gave me a very tiny smile. "You'd be surprised. I mean, didn't exactly want to do it when I was like, six. But pretty early on. My uncle was murdered when I was fourteen, and the cops bungled the case. So my family hired a PI to get to the bottom of it. And I sort of became obsessed with the idea of it. I went to school knowing that I wanted to start my own investigation company. And once I graduated, I did it."

"Holy crap," I said, too surprised at first to think of anything else to say. "Shit, I'm sorry to hear about your uncle. Did they find the guy who did it?"

She gave me a sly Cheshire Cat smile. "Course we did. I was working the case."

I just shook my head. This woman had worked her first case at fourteen—her own uncle's murder case!—and no doubt been brilliant, even then.

I'd known I was hiring a talented PI. I hadn't realized I was hiring a girl who'd actually started investigating people when she was that young.

This Charles Ray person, if he was the one stealing from us, didn't have a fucking chance against her.

And I sort of loved that.

CHAPTER 6

KATIE

THE NEXT DAY, WHEN I finally sat down in my own cubicle, I found myself very blessedly alone.

And let me tell you, it had been a long time coming. Not that I'd been at the company all that long. This was still my first week, so I couldn't exactly be running the joint yet.

But they'd put me through a hair-tearing-out amount of training in the first days of that week, and I was just about ready to scream. I definitely *would* scream if one more person thought they needed to come over and ask me to come to their desk so they could show me how to use the accounting software (completely simple) or go over the guidelines for the accounts the employees had to keep (also supremely straightforward, thank you very much).

I'd had it on the first day. I could have been running the department on the first day, if they'd let me.

Then again, I was guessing I probably had more... shall we say experience?... with alternative versions of holding information than anyone else in this department. I'd been working in tech and finance crimes for so long that I'd come up with a million different ways to learn and then keep track of new processes the moment I heard them.

So when I looked at it that way, I guessed I could probably have a little bit more patience with these people. They didn't, after all, know that they were dealing with someone who literally learned other people's systems at the drop of a hat for a living.

And speaking of which...

I looked up and turned my ears on, listening for where everyone else was in the room. I didn't have any close neighbors—they were really understaffed in this particular department—and that was actually going to make my job easier, because it meant no one would just duck around the corner of my cube without warning.

They'd have to walk to get here.

And this particular floor had been blessed with some really, *really* creaking floorboards.

Or... I mean, whatever places like this used for floorboards. I doubted they had anything to do with real wood.

Still, the point was the same. Wooden or not, that floor creaked like crazy, and I'd already noted it as the best way to determine whether anyone was coming toward me. I stood up slightly, already suspecting that I'd been mostly left alone, and peeked over the tops of the walls that made up my little slice of the room.

A quick glance through the maze of other 'slices,' and I could see that the supervisors were all busy at one of the larger desks in the corner, leaning over the desk so they could all look at the same set of paperwork. Terrific. With any luck, they were working on the same thing I was: numbers that definitely didn't add up.

Though honestly speaking, from what I'd seen, this particular department was so understaffed that they might not have noticed those numbers at all. It would certainly explain why they hadn't brought it up to the corporate office yet.

Though... I tipped my head, thinking, and cast my eyes toward the main supervisor for the department. Benjamin Stone, of Ivy League history. He had a long resume with this company, having worked his way up from the bottom, and had been head of finance for ten years.

He was the one who should have caught the numbers that didn't make sense. Why hadn't he?

Could it be that he was also involved?

My eyes slanted to the side of him, though, and took in everyone else. None of them looked any different than I would have expected. Lots of glasses and stern looks. Eyes that took in numbers quickly, and brains that did the math to turn them into other numbers.

Then again, I couldn't really expect whoever was stealing from Adam's company to be wearing a big sign that said Designated Thief.

Grinning at the thought—and sort of wishing that it was that easy—I sat back down gently in my chair, trying to avoid the creak that I'd found it *also* made. Because speaking of Adam, it was time to actually get to work.

I booted my computer in safe mode, which gave me a route to the entire company rather than just my own account, and did some quick guessing. No one was as secure as they thought they were when it came to things like account passwords, and I had an entire file on Charles Ray to give me hints.

His family. His hobbies. His pets—and their names.

Within five minutes, I was into his account and looking through his personnel data—which HR kept attached to each employee's record-keeping portal. It was neat and tidy, and also far too easy to hack into, and I made a note to talk to Adam about that. If this was their company standard, it was way too low, and that put them all at risk.

As far as what this Charles Ray was getting into... Well, his transcripts from college looked odd, to start with. There was none of the official language, no watermarks that made them look like they'd actually come from any good school—and certainly not the school he claimed they came from. I would bet my life on these being fakes, but I'd have to print them out so I could look at them more closely.

What else could I find?

I scrolled through everything, and then found the link to his actual company spending accounts.

Ah. If there was a problem, this was where I was going to find it.

I felt my lips curve up in a satisfied grin at that, and was just moving the cursor to hover over that link, read to dive in, when someone came around the corner.

"Hey, new girl!" said someone nearly shouted. "How's your first day alone in your cube?"

I jerked to attention, realizing suddenly that I'd gotten so caught up in my work that I'd forgotten to listen for those floorboards I'd been supposed to listen for, and quickly exited out of the program I was in, cursing myself for a fool and a half and then spinning around, hoping like hell that I didn't look like I'd just been sneaking through the company's personnel records.

I mean, when you looked at it that way, my first day alone in my cube had already been really, really fruitful.

But I didn't think the woman standing in front of me, all bouncy brown hair and laughing eyes to match, was going to accept that as a real answer.

"Um, you know," I stuttered. "Still trying to get my feet under me, basically. Starting a new job is always sort of like a tornado, isn't it?"

The woman with the bouncy hair gave me a sympathetic look and nodded. "Sure is, but I think I might have just the thing to help. On Friday nights, a bunch of us go out for drinks. How about joining us? It'll be the perfect way for you to get to know some of the people in the office. Outside of the actual office."

I thought about it for approximately .3 seconds. This was a good idea. I needed to make friends here if I was going to ask questions, and this woman was giving me an easy way to do it. Even better, this gave me a way to get to know people other than Adam, who I was supposed to be staying away from.

Having other friends would create a buffer between me and the guy who was actually my boss, and who had already shown a tendency to show up at my room whenever he deemed it necessary.

"Absolutely," I said firmly. "Count me in. I'm sorry, what was your name?"

The woman flashed me an enormous grin. "Rachel," she said. "Here's my number. Text me at the end of the day and I'll give you the deets!" She slid me a business card, gave me a jaunty little wave, and was then gone, leaving like the tornado I'd just compared the entire job to.

What was it with other people coming and going from my life like actual storms? Lindsey had always been a hurricane, and Adam seemed like a combination of everything: earthquake, tornado, hurricane... all wrapped up in something so hot and wet that I couldn't quite put a name to it.

Evidently I attracted intense personalities, I thought.

I looked down at the business card, considering, and then texted Adam.

Katie: *Have you heard about this drink thing they evidently do on Friday nights?*

Adam: *Sure have. I've already agreed to do it, figure it's a good idea to make friends.*

I grinned. Great minds evidently thought alike.

Katie: *Same. Guess I'll see you there.*

He just responded with a thumbs-up.

Which, I told myself firmly, was completely appropriate. It was a perfectly reasonable way to respond finish the conversation. It confirmed that we were on the same page and told me that he would, indeed, see me there.

So why did I feel sort of hollow and off-balance when I put my phone down on the desk and got to work with my tasks for the day?

⎯⎯⎯◉⎯⎯⎯

GOING OUT FOR DRINKS with so many people from the same company, it turned out, was a sort of whirlwind-slash-tornado-slash-earthquake situation in and of itself. Evidently 'a bunch of us' meant that this was some sort of known company event, and included more than just the finance or sales departments—or even *both* the sales and finance departments.

By the time I found my way to the bar that Rachel had written down for me, I counted at least thirty people I recognized milling around in the crowd, and that was only what I could see from the door.

Hey, don't judge. I'm a PI. It's my job to be able to remember faces. So being able to recognize thirty of my coworkers already—even from such a large building and company—was nothing new for me. It wasn't like I'd had to talk to these people or anything, either. They were people I'd seen in the lobby. On the stairs. Getting on and off the elevator.

And yeah, sure, some of them were from my department. But not very many of them.

If I wanted to get to know people from the company, this was definitely the way to do it.

And speaking of getting to know people from the company. It took me three seconds of staring around, somewhat dazed, to spot Rachel jumping up and down, waving at me, and then rushing toward me, two drinks in her hands.

I jerked a bit, surprised. What had she been doing, standing around with two drinks just on the off chance that she was going to need one of them when someone arrived?

"What, double-fisting already?" I asked when she arrived. "Trying to get a jump start on the night?"

She giggled, telling me clearly that she'd already had several drinks, the two in her hands notwithstanding. "No! I had this one for you, because I was just positive that you were going to show up at any moment."

I grinned, unable to stop myself. The woman was friendliness personified, and for a girl like me, who had spent life as an introvert

45

who didn't make friends easily, it was a breath of fresh air. I took the proffered drink and held it up to the light, trying to figure out what, exactly, it was.

I might be here to socialize and get to know people. That definitely didn't mean I had the time or freedom to get drunk. After all, I was still officially on the job.

"It's just a Madori sour," Rachel said, sounding apologetic. "I didn't know what you might want, and these are my favorite drinks, so I figured if you didn't show up..."

She gave me a very voluptuous—and totally unapologetic—shrug to finish the sentence, and I laughed outright.

"That," I told her, "sounds like excellent planning on your part. Lucky for me, Madori sours are one of my favorites, too." I took a sip in demonstration, and closed my eyes as the fruity, sour goodness hit my tongue. "And this one tastes perfect."

"That's what I'm always saying!" she almost shouted. "It takes a talented bartender to give it the right mix, and this place has the best ones in the city." She leaned in and dropped her voice a bit. "And believe me, I've tried all the bars, just to test that theory. Now, let's start introducing you to people. We don't get new employees that often, and everyone is just dying to meet you."

She grabbed my arm, and I was forced to follow her. Right into the tornado, I thought, shaking my head and putting on the mask I wore when I had to be social with people I didn't know.

———◦———

BY THE TIME I GOT A moment to myself again, I was pretty sure I'd met half of the company and shared drinks with them. I was feeling woozy and less-than-steady on my heels, and I was really starting to wish I'd gone back to the hotel and changed into something a whole lot more responsible, rather than coming straight from work.

Because let me tell you, drunk and wearing four-inch heels is not my idea of a good time. In fact, I don't think it's *any* woman's idea of a good time.

And don't even get me started on the fact that I'd told myself I wasn't going to be drinking enough to get drunk tonight because I needed to keep eyes and ears open.

46

What can I say? When you're an introvert and you're forced into a social situation, a little alcoholic lubrication makes the whole thing easier. And by a little, I meant...

I tried to count how many Midori sours I thought I'd had at this point, but lost track at four, and gave up, deciding instead to head for a back room and sit down for a second. It might not sober me up, but it would at least take the pressure off my feet.

I got through the bar area of the place and was just shuffling through the door to the back room I'd spotted, trying to both walk and take off my heels at the same time, when I realized that I had made a colossal mistake.

It turns out you can't walk and take off your shoes at the same time. While drunk.

I tripped on something while bending over to try to get at my shoes, and the skirt I was wearing was so tight that I didn't have the range I needed to take the step forward that would have saved me, and instead of taking off the shoe I wanted to take off, I went hurtling forward, heading right for a table with barstools attached to it.

I had a split second of panic, and then another of being grateful that no one was there to see this happen, and then hands were yanking me out of the air, saving me from the fall and bringing me upright and to a steady position.

I gasped and tried to make sense of this rapid sequence of events—and the fact that I was standing upright rather than lying on the ground, the way I'd thought I was going to be, and finally looked up to find the laughing chocolate eyes of Adam Miller staring me right in the face.

"Careful," he said, unable to control his grin. "This the first time you've walked in those shoes, or...?"

"The first time I've tried to do it after I've had an unknown number of Midori sours," I admitted, grinning wryly.

He gave me an impressed look. "Unknown number? For you? That must be pretty high."

I just shrugged helplessly. "Honestly, I don't know. Rachel gave me one and then took me around to introduce me to everyone in the bar, and I kept saying yes to more drinks, and..."

I shook my head at my own foolishness, but Adam just kept grinning like a maniac.

When he leaned in and his face got conspiratorial, I realized—
from the smell of him—that he'd probably had a few himself.

"To be honest, I don't know how many I've had, either. Does
that make me a bad person?"

I tapped my lips like I was actually thinking about it. "I don't
know. If it does, I guess it makes me a bad person, too, and I'm not
sure I want to admit that."

He giggled in a very un-CEO-like manner, but then grew serious.
"Stick out your tongue," he demanded.

I cringed, confused. "Excuse me?"

"Stick. Out. Your. Tongue," he said, enunciating each word very
clearly. "Go on. Let's see it."

Ah. The tongue thing. He wanted to see whether my tongue was
green or not. I knew it wouldn't be—as I had, in fact, been enjoying
a green apple candy when I told him that Midori sours turned your
tongue green—but I didn't have the heart to tell him no.

I did, however, make a horrendous face when I stuck my tongue
out at him. Just like a three-year-old facing her arch enemy.

He reached out and dabbed one finger right onto my tongue. "I
knew it!" he crowed. "Not green! Not green at all!"

I snatched my tongue back, surprised, but he didn't take his hand
back. Instead, he slipped it up under my chin, and then around my
jaw, wrapping his fingers through my hair like he was about to draw
me in for a kiss.

And dammit, did I ever want him to.

Everything around us went completely still and quiet, like the
world itself had paused in its spinning, everyone out in the bar
frozen in some child's game of tag, and I felt the breath still in my
lungs. The air around me go sluggish with anticipation.

The tornado that had been brewing between us to start sparking
with lightning.

Then he shook himself, like he'd just realized what he was
doing, and let go of me.

And the world started spinning again. Complete with the rules
I'd set for myself.

"Um, we should probably get back," I stuttered. "Not together,
though. Don't want anyone thinking we came back here together to
make out or something." I forced a grin at that, like I was telling a

joke rather than picturing what would have happened if that was exactly what we'd done. "I'll go first, okay?"

He cleared his throat and stuck his hands in his pockets. "Yeah. Of course. That sounds great. We'll do a meeting tomorrow, if that's okay with you. I'll talk to you then."

I murmured something about that sounding great, then turned and fled the back room, and all the temptation it held, for safer—and louder and more crowded—quarters.

CHAPTER 7

ADAM

I DIDN'T SLEEP MUCH that night, and it wasn't only because I never sleep well when I've had too much to drink.

It was a lot more about not being able to get my fucking brain to stop whirling around, feeding me every image I'd ever had of Katie Walters, and then finishing off with a whole range of options for what might have happened in the bar if I hadn't let go of her and taken three steps back the moment I realized what I was doing.

Because I swear on everything holy that I'd had only one thing on my mind in that moment: leaning forward, tightening my grip on her hair, and sealing my mouth to hers. Figuring out exactly what she tasted like when she'd had too many Midori sours, and finding out whether she wanted to kiss me as badly as I wanted to kiss her.

I made a silent promise to thank the Midori gods at some point, if I ever got the chance, and turned over, squinting into the sun shining through the window of my hotel room.

Thank goodness it was Saturday. Thank goodness I didn't have anything I had to do today aside from organize the files for our case and see if I saw any patterns there that we might have missed in the past.

Then I remembered that I'd told Katie we were going to have a meeting today about those very files and rolled quickly out of bed—holding my head as I did so—and made my way to the shower. In my experience, only one thing helped a hangover, and that was a big, very greasy breakfast.

I wanted to get to it so I could get my brain moving and get ready for that meeting. And the girl I'd spent all night thinking about.

<hr>

OF COURSE, THE MOMENT I got into the shower, my brain went right back to Katie. I wondered what she was doing right now. In the shower, herself? Would she be up, yet? Or was she still sleeping?

Still spread across the bed, that gorgeous chestnut hair of hers draped over the edge of it, her face relaxed with sleep, her mouth slightly open...

"Fuck," I groaned as I felt the blood rushing right from my head to my cock at the thought of her in bed. I imaged her lying there naked, those curves, which I'd only seen because of the way her clothes hugged her body, bare to the world. Maybe just covered by a sheet. One of those translucent ones that left very little to the imagination. I imaged walking through the door and seeing her that way, then stripping as I walked toward her. Slipping that sheet off her body and crawling on top of her with nothing on my mind but figuring out whether her skin tasted as sweet as it looked. I closed my eyes, the better to imagine it, and slid my hand down my body, taking my now rock-hard cock in my hand and starting to rub it.

"Fuckkk," I gasped.

I was so hard already that I was about to explode, and I'd just been *thinking* about the girl. What would happen if I actually got to touch her? Run my hands up over those hips and wrap my fingers around her breasts. Spread her legs with my knee, then look down and admire how wet she was for me. Get up between her legs, slide the tip of my cock right through her dark curls and up against her center.

I gasped, my hand moving faster and faster on my cock, taking in the whole thing now and coming up over the tip because I knew how I reacted to that, and slammed my other hand against the wall of the shower to support myself.

Then I went back to my daydream. Back to the idea of sliding the head of my cock into her opening just to hear her gasp. Watching her hands clutch the pillows. Watching her toss her head back and groan for me, her tits pushing up into the sky.

I'd lie down over her, then, put my lips to those pink nipples. Biting, sucking, driving her wild.

"Fuck!" The orgasm took me by surprise, thundering down my spine and through my pelvis without any warning, and a second later I was groaning and straining against it, every single piece of my brain focused on the pleasure between my legs as I came all over the wall of the shower.

Wishing it was her. Wishing she was here in front of me right now, her hands on my ass and my hands buried in her hair.

"Dammit," I moaned with a shudder, leaning against the wall.

That hadn't been why I'd gotten into the shower. It hadn't been anywhere in my mind. But that girl... That girl hit me in a place no one had ever touched. Smart and almost too clever for her own good, she was also hands-down the most beautiful woman I'd ever laid eyes on.

And she could match me when it came to how quick she was. I'd never even thought about it, but that was the final straw. I didn't know many people who could keep up with me.

Finding a woman who could not only match me but probably beat me when it came to her wits was so hot that I couldn't keep her out of my mind.

And the fact that she was forbidden made it even hotter. The woman was basically my employee, for shit's sake, and every professional bone in my body knew that I absolutely had to keep my hands off of her.

The bone currently in my hand, however, thought that her being forbidden fruit just made her even sexier.

It was something I was definitely going to have to tamp down before I saw her again. Because I wasn't going to take that step. No matter how fucking sexy and smart she was.

⸻⬤⸻

I GOT OUT OF MY SHOWER, knees still a little shaky, to find my phone ringing, and rushed toward it, going through the very tricky process of answering a cell phone when your hands are still damp.

"Hello?" I asked breathlessly.

"Damn, what are you doing, running a marathon down there?" Oliver asked, his voice colored with a smile. Then his voice went breathless, too. "Or were you expecting someone else to call? Someone who deserved a sexy tone of voice?"

I grinned, just because it was impossible to take Oliver seriously when he decided to become ridiculous. "Shut it, Oliver. I ran in here from the other room. What's up?"

"Just a weekly check-in, boss. Nothing to report from the home camp, but I thought you might have interesting news for me. How's it going down there? Find anything useful yet?"

Aside from the fact that my PI is the sexiest woman I've ever met and my entire body wants to pin her against the wall and have my way with her?

I didn't say that part out loud, though. That was none of Oliver's business, and I knew him well enough to know that telling him something that was a virtual guarantee that it would be all over the office by this time Monday morning.

He was my best friend. He also sucked at keeping his mouth shut.

"We've only been here a week, but we've already got some good leads, and Katie is phenomenal at her job," I said. "She's been into a couple of personnel files and has some people of interest. We're having a meeting about our progress today, actually."

"Ah, the infamous private investigator," he said, his voice turning sly. "Katie, is it? And is she as perky and optimistic as her name indicates?"

I felt a frown cross over my face, though I didn't stop to think about it much. "I wouldn't call her perky *or* optimistic, honestly. More like an insanely smart librarian-slash-engineer who can outthink just about anyone on the planet, from what I've seen."

"Sounds like she's just the person for the job, then," Oliver said quickly. "A perfect fit."

"You could say that," I agreed. "She's managed to figure out how the office is handling their passwords already, and has pinpointed some big holes in their processes, according to the email she sent me. And it took her about five minutes to do it. Before we leave, she's going to have rewritten all of their security protocols."

I laughed, amused—and pleased—at how quickly she'd sorted things out, and I was surprised when I only heard silence on the other end of the phone.

"Oliver?" I asked. "Did you hear me?"

"Yeah, I heard you," he said quickly. "Um, that's great, but I've just gotten an email that I have to take care of. Do you mind if we pick this back up later?"

Okay, that was weird. *He* was the one who'd called *me*. And what was he doing answering emails at—I checked the clock—7 on a Saturday morning?

"Sure, that's fine. You don't need to call me back, actually. I haven't got anything to report yet."

Oliver didn't even say goodbye. He just hung up the phone, leaving me staring at it for several long moments as I tried to figure out what was wrong with him. He should have been all over Katie finding holes in Houston's programs. He was the head of finance.

He should have been asking for notes.

Then I realized that he could also just be telling the truth. I'd left him in charge of the office back in New York, and it was more responsibility than he was used to. He was probably just taking it really seriously.

And I was probably just being paranoid because my best friend had almost caught me taking my dog for a walk while thinking about the girl I'd hired to find out whether there was anything mysterious going on in my company.

I shook my head at myself, told myself once again to get myself under control, and went to get dressed, wondering when I could get that girl—who was the one girl in the world I legitimately couldn't have—on the phone for the meeting I'd promised her.

CHAPTER 8

KATIE

I WAS NOT FEELING WELL.

But I knew—or had, at least, been told by the infamous Lindsey—that the best thing to do for a hangover was go have breakfast. Preferably something salty.

At least I thought that was what she'd said. Though now that I was trying to remember, I couldn't quite recall. Probably because I hadn't been listening very closely to her at the time.

Which was probably because I'd never in one million and three years thought I'd be in a position to need that sort of information.

The state of my stomach this morning said otherwise, though, and no matter how much I wracked my brain for that freaking information, I couldn't quite get to it. I remembered the conversation, I remembered thinking that I would probably never use the advice and wondering exactly how much Lindsey'd had to drink before she came up with this particular equation.

But no matter how hard I tried, I couldn't hear what she'd actually told me to eat.

Of course, that could have been because my head felt like it was full of fluff at the moment.

Still, knowing that food was probably the best possible cure—if for no other reason than to soak up any alcohol still remaining in my stomach—I stumbled out of my room after a long, very hot shower, and got onto the elevator.

The feel of it dropping out from under my feet made me even sicker.

Shit, I hoped food would help.

The thing that didn't help was the elevator coming to a pause a couple floors down, the doors opening, and Adam Miller strolling in like he freaking owned the joint.

Oh my freakin' goodness. I felt like I was going to either faint or throw up, and now I had to share an elevator with Adam Miller. Who was going to see me in this kind of shape.

Wait. I had a flash of a memory of him from last night. A flash that put him right in front of me, his fingers on my jaw, his face only inches from mine as we stared into each other's eyes like we were in some sort of slow-motion montage.

Oh fuckity-fuck. I hadn't kissed him, had I? What happened at the end of that memory? Shit, shit, shit.

I throttled my brain, trying to get it to go past that one flash of a scene, but couldn't seem to get it to function. There was nothing after that. No kiss. No memory of safely walking away.

Wait. Was that memory even real?

It was. I was sure of it. The sudden fluttering in my stomach at his presence told me so.

He gave me one quick look up and down, and shook his head. "You look almost as good as me this morning."

I gave him a crooked smile. "Is that a compliment or an insult?"

He smiled back and walked forward to press the button and get the elevator to start moving again. "Neither. Just an observation that I'm guessing we both could have done with a little bit less to drink last night."

"You can say that again," I moaned. "I never want to see another Midori sour for as long as I live. Longer, if possible. If they have them in heaven, I'm turning around and walking back out again."

He sputtered with laughter, though I noticed that it was a lot more muted than it had been. I was guessing that was because his head felt like it might roll right off his body at any moment.

"Girl refuses to go to heaven because of Midori sours," he intoned, making it obvious that he was making up a title from a newspaper story. "Opts for hell, where they only drink whiskey."

"Oh my goodness, don't mention alcohol to me again for the rest of the weekend," I returned. "Or I'm going to have to walk out on you. Where are you going, anyhow?"

"Breakfast," he said with a grin. "I've always heard a big, greasy breakfast is the best thing for a hangover."

"That's it!" I muttered.

He tipped his head. "That's what?"

"I was trying to remember what my friend had said you should eat after you've had too much to drink," I admitted. "But I wasn't really paying attention to the conversation, and I hadn't recorded it. I was guessing something salty. It actually sounds better."

He put up his hands as a set of scales, and moved them up and down. "I mean, salty, greasy, what's the difference? Doesn't one go with the other?"

"Exactly," I agreed. "Which means I was right about the salty part."

"I didn't think we were having a competition, but I'll give you that one," he noted solemnly. The elevator dinged, then, and came to a halt, the doors rolling open. He offered me his arm, the perfect gentleman. "Shall we go to breakfast, my lady?"

I took his arm, but gave him a very jaded look. "As long as you don't call me that ever again. It makes me sound like an old woman."

He raised the hand that wasn't currently holding my arm, like he was taking an oath. "I do solemnly swear to never again call you my lady. On my honor. For my entire life."

"Thank you," I said primly. "Now, let's go find food. And pray that this magical remedy works."

Which was how we ended up walking into the dining room together, our arms linked and our heads bowed together as we discussed what we were going to eat first, and how we were going to measure whether it actually helped with a hangover or not. By the time we were seated, we'd each decided on the ingredients for our relatively large breakfast, and were already prepared to order when the waiter arrived.

"Orange juice," I told him, without waiting. "And coffee. Sausage, hash browns, eggs, and plenty of toast. Please."

"I'll take the same. And add two plates of pancakes," Adam added. "Also, French toast."

I glanced at him, surprised at the sheer amount of food, and he just shrugged and grinned bashfully. "I figure as long as we're going for it, we might as well go all in. Right? And honestly, who doesn't like French toast? It should be a freebie with every meal."

"Only if it comes with cinnamon sugar," I replied. "None of that powdered sugar, and definitely no syrup. Or fruit spread."

He picked up his glass and lifted it for a toast. When I lifted mine as well and clinked them together, he nodded.

"To a land where French toast is free for everyone, and only comes with cinnamon sugar," he said solemnly. "If I were president, I would make it so."

"A land where the French toast is free," I said, trying hard to suppress the smile I could feel growing on my lips. "It sounds like such a magical place."

He leaned forward, his chin dropping and his eyes going all dreamy. "I would create that sort of place for you. I would make sure you lived in a world where you could have all the French toast you wanted, and only the toppings you liked."

The breath fled my body at that, and the world did that weird slowing-down thing again, until it was only him and me, caught in some sort of weird time warp that blurred the rest of reality until it didn't matter.

I leaned forward too, fighting through the sudden tension of the table, and got as close as I dared before I whispered, "Can you add cheesecake? Just for a little variety?"

And at that, the spell was broken. As I'd hoped it would be.

Because neither of us could afford to let this little flirtation get out of hand. Sure, I wanted to take him to bed and lick him up and down like a freaking Adam popsicle. See exactly how those fingers could touch me. Revel in the feeling of his hard, strong body against me as he took me again and again.

But I didn't have that option. The man was a client. And I didn't sleep with people I was working for.

He backed up several inches, his eyes growing a bit cooler. "Cheesecake is definitely doable," he noted. "I didn't realize you were a fan."

"I could quite happily live on cheesecake," I said simply.

And at that moment, our breakfasts arrived, and we dug in, moving the conversation over to the case at hand and the man we thought might actually be responsible for the missing money. Adam was having Oliver, his best friend and right-hand man, look into that man's employment record and hiring paperwork, to see whether anything had looked weird, and I was going to dive back into his personal records once we got back in the office.

For the moment, it was the best we could do.

But we could stay here as long as we needed to and keep digging. As long as we didn't get caught first.

As long as we didn't mess it up by allowing the heat between us to turn into something bigger and more real.

59

CHAPTER 9

ADAM

"I REALLY THINK THIS program could help you out with that," I told the client I had on the phone. "It'll track all your social media activity *and* tell you how many people you're reaching *and* tell you whether they're clicking through on your links or just deleting the email. And as any good business owner knows, those click-throughs are where it's at, am I right?"

Dana Carver, the owner of a number of salons in the Houston area, huffed out a laugh. "You've got that right. It's amazing how many people don't know that, though. They think that if you're getting email out to people, that's all you need to do. They don't realize that unless people follow through on that email..."

"It's completely pointless," I agreed. "They're reading your material but they're not paying you for it, essentially, and they're certainly not doing your business any favors. So what if I could tell you that we also offer a service that actually writes those emails for you—which saves you a ton of time—and specializes in making sure you actually get those click-throughs?"

There was a short pause, but I was 99 percent sure I already had her on the hook. Dana had grown her business too quickly, and was no struggling with several of her salons having half-empty sales. She needed to drive business to those salons. And as far as I could see, some of our more straightforward marketing strategies and programs were the perfect answer for her.

I just had to make her see that.

"Click-throughs would be amazing," she finally said. "What do you need from me?"

I grinned and took her through the steps I'd recommend, then took down her email and promised her that I'd be emailing her all the information I had at my fingertips within the next five minutes.

"Look into some of these programs, and before you know it, you're going to need to open a whole range of new salons just to take care of the business we'll be sending your way," I told her, grinning.

I could hear the returning grin when she answered. "You, Adam, are a freaking lifesaver. How do you know so much about running a business, anyhow? You've answered all the questions I didn't even know I had."

I opened my mouth to answer, to tell her that I'd gone through the same questions when I was opening the company, and that I'd actually created the answers myself—and then realized that if they'd worked for me, then they would work for other people too, and should become part of our line.

Then I snapped my mouth shut. Because I wasn't supposed to know any of that. I wasn't Adam Miller right now, but Adam Jones, lowly sales guy who knows the outlines of the company but definitely didn't know the inner workings. I certainly wouldn't know what Adam Miller had gone through trying to get Miller and Co off the ground.

I would never have had access to that sort of information.

"I've been working with businesses for a long time," I lied smoothly—although technically, it wasn't really a lie. "I know what clients are looking for, and I've gone through our offerings enough times that I know exactly what works for people like you. It's what makes me a great representative. I'm working for both you and Miller."

Damn, that was a good line, and I'd totally come up with it on the fly. I should incorporate that into the marketing material somewhere. Make it the headline on some of our brochures.

Gina chuckled. "Well, if there's a place for me to leave a review, you let me know. I've never worked with a salesman who understood business so well, and I've got to say, it's refreshing."

"That is very good to hear," I said, feeling a thrill of pride run through me.

Hey, hearing that you're doing a good job never gets old. I'd been CEO of Miller for going on seven years, now, and I still liked getting the random compliment. It shored up your confidence. Made you feel like you were doing a good job.

Put a grin on your face.

"Now, I'm going to email you right now, so sit tight and let me now when you get it, okay?"

She agreed, and I hung up the phone feeling nearly as excited as I had when I made my first sale seven years ago. That high, it turned out, never got old.

"I've got to say, you've definitely got a knack with the clients," a voice said from directly behind me.

I jerked to attention and whirled around, shocked that someone was so close to me, and that I hadn't even noticed. I found the person who had spoken even closer than I realized, too.

James Andrews, the supervisor of my department, was actually sitting in the spare chair I kept in my cube, his elbows leaning on his knees like he was about to tell me some secret.

"Uh, yeah," I answered smoothly. "I, uh... I mean, there's a reason I chose this as my career." I finally got myself back on track at that point and gave him a quick smile. "I learned pretty early on that the best way to get a client on your side is to give them the answers they didn't even know they were looking for, and then make them think it was their idea in the first place. It's never let me down."

He chuckled and nodded. "I'm starting to think I should have you teach everyone else in this department about it. You sure seem to have a more straightforward route than anyone else."

Uh oh. He was looking at me now like he wondered how I had so much experience when I was still relatively young. And the last thing I needed was him asking questions like that.

"Well, I've done quite a bit of job hopping, so I've had a chance to learn from a lot of different people," I said quickly, using the first excuse that came to mind. "So, you know, that's helped."

He relaxed a bit, and I breathed a sigh of relief. "I did see that on your resume. You've been at quite a few different companies. Any particular reason you've been jumping around?"

Shit, what was this, the Spanish Inquisition? Did this guy grill all of his new employees like this?

More likely, I realized, he just grilled the ones who came in and outsold everyone else in their first week on the job.

Shit, I should have been a whole lot more subtle than that. I'd jumped right into the deep end, though, putting all my tricks and magic to work for me right from the start, and now I realized how fucking stupid that had been. I was just supposed to be a salesman. Not a guy who looked like he could be running the company.

Shit, shit, shit.

I shrugged, trying to play it off. "Took a long time for me to get to a company that I felt fit me, honestly. I can tell you, though, that Miller feels like it might be the place. I'm into the tech, and I love the marketing. Plus, the culture here feels..."

I paused, searching for the work, and James jumped right in—as I'd hoped he would.

"Close," he said quickly. "Like family. We work hard on that, and let me tell you, being in Texas makes it easier. Everyone here feels like they could be related. Have you gone out for drinks with everyone yet?"

"Everyone is right," I chuckled. "I thought it would be ten people, twenty, max! Not the entire company."

He beamed with pride, like the drinks thing had been his idea in the first place. "Family," he confirmed. "And it gets better the longer you've been here. Stop by my office sometime this week, Adam. I'd love to take you to lunch. Pick your brain about some of your sales activity." He paused and tipped his head. "You sure do know a lot for someone so young. And I can't get over the feeling that I know you from somewhere."

Double shit with rainbow sprinkles, we were back to him recognizing me now?

I forced a laugh. "I'm telling you, it's my face. It's just enough like so many other people that I'm constantly recognized as someone I most definitely am not."

James shook his head. "I have a friend who's the same way. Stop by my office this week, let's get lunch."

And he ambled off without saying anything else.

I watched him go, biting my lip. James was the supervisor here, so it was his job to keep an eye on his employees. But if he kept snooping on me, we were going to have a very big problem.

I couldn't afford to be caught undercover in my own company. It would be a huge embarrassment, to start with, and finding out that I was going incognito in the different offices would absolutely send anyone stealing money underground.

Or make them more careful, and therefore harder to catch.

I had to be more careful. And Katie had to work a whole lot faster on figuring out who was stealing money in this office, so we could get the hell out of here before we were caught. Because neither of us was going to get out of this without some serious damage, if anyone figured out what we were doing.

⎯⎯⎯◉⎯⎯⎯

"WE'VE GOT TO FIGURE out who's stealing the money before my boss figures out why I look familiar to him," I said the moment Katie opened the door to her hotel room.

She lifted both eyebrows as high as they would go and looked me up and down, then frowned and looked to the right and left, up and down the hallway.

"Is that how you greet every girl who opens a door? Because I've got to say, it leaves a whole lot to be desired."

I'd thought she was maybe going to just stand around making jokes and flirting, but instead, she grabbed my arm and yanked me through the door, then basically shoved me into the living room of her suite.

"It also runs a really high risk of blowing your cover. Have you even considered that saying things like that will get you found out and out discovered, and it'll be no one's fault but your own? Have you thought that maybe you should work at least a little bit harder on keeping your mouth shut rather than acting like you own the entire company and can say whatever you want?"

I hadn't. But I was considering that pretty carefully right now.

She watched me go through that realization, and shook her head, the ultimate professional in the face of a rookie—which I hadn't been in years.

"Just watch what you say when we're in public places," she said. "Or you'll definitely out us to the nearest Miller employee. And it seems to me that's exactly what you're trying to avoid. What's the problem with your boss?"

"He thinks he recognizes me," I said quickly, moving over and sitting down on the sofa. "And he's under the impression that I'm selling more than anyone else in the department."

At that, she gave me a truly unbelieving look. "And... *have* you been selling more than anyone else in the department?"

I hung my head. "I haven't *not* been selling, if that's what you're asking."

And now she just shook her head, thoroughly disappointed in my inability to sneak around. "You'd think this was the first time you'd gone undercover," she noted.

"Well, to be honest, it is," I retorted. "I don't exactly do this for a living."

She repressed a smile at that, and my body eased at the realization that she was mostly just teasing me.

"Okay, all that aside, what do you have for me?" she asked, sitting down at the desk and looking for all the world like she was preparing to start taking notes. Despite the fact that she was in yoga pants and a sweatshirt.

"I called Oliver earlier to ask what he'd found out about this Charles Ray person," I said, transitioning smoothly into the real reason I'd come to her room.

Because I'd come to talk about Charles Ray. And James Andrews. And I didn't want to do it over the phone, in case someone was listening in. I'd also found that brainstorming went best when you did it in person.

I'm serious.

It had absolutely zero to do with wanting to see her.

"He says the vetting process was clean on him. The interview process was complete, and all of his references checked out."

Katie narrowed her eyes. "And yet his college transcripts are faked. I noticed that they looked wrong when I was going through his files, and I called the college to confirm. They don't have any record of a Charles Ray going to school there. Much less graduating."

I narrowed my eyes at that, too. "That doesn't make sense. Why would Oliver say the process had gone fine if he was coming around with faked transcripts? Come to that, why would the process have gone fine if his transcripts were faked? Shouldn't someone have checked on that?"

We stared at each other for several long moments, both of us going through the mental mazes that those questions brought up.

Damn, she was beautiful, I realized suddenly. All chestnut hair and green eyes and lush lips and broad cheekbones and...

My eyes flicked to those lips, and I licked my own at the thought of tasting hers. Then I remembered what I'd done earlier in the shower, and felt the blood go rushing to my cheeks.

When I looked up again, her eyes were still sealed to mine. But they'd changed, going darker and somehow more suggestive. Her gaze turned down to my lips, considering, and then came back to mine.

Dammit it to hell! Man, did I want to kiss that women. Pull her against me and figure out whether her curves fit with mine as well as I thought they would. Run my fingers over her skin, bring up goosebumps, and then kiss them away.

And the crazy thing was, I saw her thinking exactly the same thing.

Then we both jerked, remembering where—and who—we were, and turned away.

"Anyhow, that's all I really have right now," I muttered.

"Yeah," she said, shuffling her papers. "Well, something's not matching up. He faked those transcripts, and we need to figure out why. He's the closest thing we've got to a lead right now, so I'm going back into his files tomorrow to see what else I can find."

Our gazes clashed again, the sparks flying through the air, and I got out of the chair and started walking toward the door.

"Terrific. He's in my department, so I'll try to make contact with him. See if he acts as suspicious as he seems."

"Um, perfect," she said from behind me. "I'll see you tomorrow, then."

I got through the door without having to say anything else and slammed it shut, then leaned up against it, my cock growing long and starting to ache.

That woman was trouble. And if I didn't get this case finished and get myself home to New York soon, then I was going to create a situation that I didn't think I could pull myself out of.

I pushed myself off the door and made for my own hotel room, my mind already on another shower. A cold one, this time.

CHAPTER 10

KATIE

I WALKED RIGHT TO THE door Adam had just gone through, threw the lock to make sure he didn't somehow come back in to cause more trouble, and leaned my forehead against the wooden—because this was a really expensive hotel—surface, taking in the cool smoothness of it and trying to apply that smoothness to my own mind.

When that didn't work—because of course it wouldn't—I stalked into the bathroom, leaned on the counter, and stared at my reflection in the mirror.

"Woman," I told myself firmly, "you have got to get yourself under control. You're here to do a job. You're here to track down and stop the money leaks in his company. He's hired you because of your reputation for hard work. If you had a reputation as someone who slept with the people who hired her, he would not have hired you. No one would hire you ever again. You've already worked too hard, as a woman, to get ahead in this field, and you're not going to throw it all away for a pretty face. You. Have. Got. To. Get. Yourself. Under. Control."

I leaned even further in and stared myself in the eye, taking in the mild green color, the flecks of gold and darker green, and the glare there that told me I meant business.

Because I was telling Mirror Katie the truth. I couldn't screw this up. I had a very successful company and a very solid reputation for good work. I ran good numbers and did especially well when I was dealing with difficult, shady cases. I had never disappointed a client.

And I had never slept with any of them, either.

I didn't even feel like I should have to say that, honestly. That should just be a given.

Anyhow, the point was the same: I'd never slept with a client before, and I wasn't going to start now. Even if Adam Miller was the very definition of smolder, with his dark eyes and dark hair, the

67

stubble I wanted to brush my cheek against, and those glasses, which I knew were fake, but which still gave him the look of being some sort of emo hunk.

I just had to take the buzzing in my veins, the deep ache between my legs, and put them away for the next week.

And one more thing. I needed to get this case settled so I could get home before I did anything to screw up the reputation I'd worked so hard and so long for.

I gave Mirror Katie one last long, hard look, and then turned and left the bathroom, heading straight for my phone—and the only person I could count on to tell me the truth no matter what.

"Lindsey," I muttered when she answered the phone. "I'm in trouble."

She didn't even pause. "Oh my goodness, it's finally happened, hasn't it? You've finally done something to get in trouble with the mafia. I didn't even know they had a branch in Houston. What did you do? Did you see one of their hits? Have they already put a hit out on you? Do they have guys chasing you in dark suits and sunglasses and greasy hair? Is there—"

"Lindsey!" I interrupted. "It's not the mafia. Damn, woman. Get your imagination under control, please."

I could almost see her huffing in disappointment at that. Look, Lindsey was one of the most honest people I knew. But she also had the heart of a romantic, and she was *obsessed* with the mob. When I first decided to go into private investigation, literally the first question she'd asked me was whether I'd be investigating the mob. And I thought she probably hoped with at least half of her heart that every case I took would end up involving Italian men who shouted a whole lot and all had New York Italian accents.

Even if it meant my life would be in danger.

"What's going on, then?" she asked, sounding slightly disappointed. "Are you okay? Are you safe?"

"I'm fine," I grumbled. "If you call nearly kissing the man who hired me—twice—fine."

This time when Lindsey answered me, she was very clearly grinning so hard she could hardly contain it. "You almost kissed him?" she squealed. "Twice? Why didn't you? What happened? Give me details, woman!"

I sighed. This wasn't what I'd been hoping for when I called her for an honest opinion of how bad it would be if I had kissed him. This was a whole lot more like telling a fan of a certain boy band that I'd had a run-in with a member of that boy band and had actually gotten his phone number.

Only we weren't fourteen, and we weren't talking about boy bands. We were talking about my client. A very good one, and one that I couldn't afford to mess around with.

Still, I went quickly through the rough details of what had happened in the bar, and then again in my room. "I can't do anything with him," I said, finishing the story. "If I did, I'd ruin my reputation. and you know how hard I've worked to establish myself. I've already had to fight an uphill battle as a woman in a man's world. It would destroy the company if it got around that I was sleeping with clients."

Lindsey paused, and this time I could imagine her pulling herself back. Getting a hold of that insane attraction she seemed to have for the man who was currently my boss and trying to impose some practicality on her romantic streak. When she spoke, she wasn't grinning anymore. "You're right. This would completely kill your company. You can't do anything. But I don't think you need me to tell you that. Surely you already know it. So why did you call?"

"Just to have someone confirm it for me," I said with a sigh. "I know it. I do. But it's getting awfully hard to remember it. I need someone to tell me exactly what will happen if I follow through on it."

"Nothing good," she said sharply, and here was the Lindsey I'd called to talk to. Here was the practical, no-nonsense side of my best friend. The one who would handcuff you to the dresser if it meant keeping you from hurting yourself. "You obviously can't take the chance. Are you going to be able to finish the case?"

And now we felt like we were back on solid footing again. "I have to," I told her firmly. "I need that bounty. And..."

"And you like him," she guessed. "You don't want to disappoint him, and you don't want to leave him high and dry. But you have to get this case done quickly, before you screw something up by getting too friendly with him."

"Exactly," I said with a wry grin.

"And how close are you to solving the case?"

"Not. That's the problem. We have a suspect, but nothing firm. I'm going into the system for more information on him, but there aren't exactly any glaring, red, neon signs pointing to him as the guy. Just some weird stuff with his background."

Lindsey was quiet for a long moment, then said, "Right, well, I guess you'll just have to keep searching. Get someone that Adam can look at harder, figure out how they're doing it, plug up the holes they were using, and then get the hell out of there and get to a safer case. Right?"

"I couldn't have said it better myself. And what do I tell Adam in the meantime?"

"You don't tell him anything. You make sure you're not alone with him, you make damn sure you don't give him any openings, and you absolutely, positively don't kiss him. Then you get his number and send it to me, because there's no rule against *me* kissing him, and I'm currently in the market for a kissing partner."

I laughed at that, my stress rising up off my shoulders and flitting out the window at the joke, and by the time I got off the phone with her, I had a new plan of action and the feeling that it would definitely work.

Tomorrow, I was going to go into the office, find Charles Ray, and try to nail him down. I was going to close this case as quickly as I could so I could get home—and away from Adam Miller.

And, if possible, I was going to get Adam's number and pass it to Lindsey for *her* to stalk him in all her free time.

I put my phone down, carefully segmenting my brain so that I didn't think about how I actually felt about this plan, and went back to work on those files, trying to find a pattern in when Charles Ray went to lunch and took his breaks.

<hr>

I WALKED INTO THE BREAK room at exactly 10:20, which, according to my research, was when Charles generally logged out of the system and went for a coffee refill. I walked casually, also carrying a coffee mug, and though I was on the wrong floor, my department being on the 7th floor rather than the 5th, which housed sales, I had an excuse all prepared.

I was down here to pass some paperwork to the head of the finance department, and I'd brought my coffee mug because I was probably going to be here for a while. As such, I'd come to the break room seeking a refill.

Easy peasy. Totally natural, totally believable.

"Oops, I'm sorry," I said as I placed myself closer to Charles than was necessary and hit his hip with the open drawer. "This isn't my break room and I'm looking for those cute little creamers. Do you know if they have any in here?"

He scooted to the side but seemed to buy my excuse, because he grinned at me in a slightly condescending way. "We don't use those, but we have a big selection in the fridge over there," he said. "I think someone somewhere decided that the little creamers weren't very efficient. Plus, all that plastic waste."

"Oh my gosh, you're totally right," I said, putting on my best and most practiced airhead mask. "I'm still getting used to the way this company runs. The company I used to work for had a ton of those little things. Enough that I used to grab some of them and take them home for myself."

I added this last part in a whisper, like I was telling him a secret, and it totally worked. He ducked toward me as well, his lips curving up in a smile.

"I've done the same thing. Don't worry. I won't tell anyone."

I let out a bright, charming laugh. "I don't work there anymore, so I'm not sure you could tell anyone who mattered."

Now he really looked at me, letting his eyes travel up and down my body once. "So you're one of the new people they just brought in? We have a new guy on this floor, too. You all came from corporate?"

Right, here was the tricky part. Because if he was really our guy, then he absolutely couldn't know why we'd come from corporate.

"Sure did," I said, still bright and charming and fairly brainless. "I guess they've been collecting the resumes of people who've applied to different branches in the past, and just use them to fill in holes when they have them."

It worked, too. He nodded as if this made total sense and went back to making his own coffee. "Still, you'd think there were enough people in the market for a job that they wouldn't have any trouble hiring."

Got him.

"You'd think so, but I think there are a lot of people who are lying about things these days, to get jobs they maybe don't deserve. You know, faking their resumes. Using falsified college degrees and records. Saying they have education they don't have."

I was watching him when I said it, so I saw his shoulders suddenly rise up in tension, his face grow tight with stress.

Double got him.

I hadn't had any doubt about the records I'd found—or about the phone call I'd made to the college he'd claimed to go to—but if I had, his intense and sudden defensiveness made it all too clear that this man was hiding something.

Something to do with his college transcripts. And if I was right, then that meant he was hiding other things, too.

I just needed to find out how he was doing it.

"Anyhow," I said quickly. "I have to run. Thanks for the tip about the creamers! What was your name again?"

He turned toward me, all charm gone from his expression. "Um, Charles," he said, his voice a little bit hoarse. "I work in sales."

I pretended not to notice the change in tone. "Katie," I said, grinning. "From finance. I'll see you around, Charles."

I didn't wait for him to answer. I didn't need to. He'd already told me all I needed to know.

The man was hiding things. And I was going to find out what they were.

⸻⸻◉⸻⸻

I GOT BACK TO MY HOTEL room, almost jumping out of my skin with excitement about telling Adam that I'd made contact with our suspect.

When I texted him, though, he texted back saying that he had a conference call that he couldn't miss, and that he'd have to talk to me tomorrow.

Now, on the surface, this was no big deal. The information could certainly keep until tomorrow, and it made sense that Adam had to do a conference call. I mean, he was still the CEO of a multi-billion-dollar corporation.

But the idea of not talking to him, after I'd talked to him every day for the past week, and instead just having dinner on my own...

Felt wrong. It felt empty, to be more specific.

It shouldn't have. I shouldn't have cared. The fact that I did made me very, very nervous.

CHAPTER 11

KATIE

"LINDSEY, I NEED HELP."

"Oh shit, what now? Wait, the mafia? Is it the mafia? Did they finally find you?"

Dammit, the girl had a one-track mind. No wonder she was a great teacher. I mean, aside from the fact that she was a total party girl on the weekends, which did *not* go with teaching first grade, she had an ability to focus unlike anyone I'd ever met.

Unfortunately, there were times when she focused on the wrong thing.

"No, as much as it might shock you, the mafia is still not involved in my current case," I told her with a straight face. "But if they decide to come in and take over, my first call will be to you. I might be tied up and in the trunk of an unmarked sedan, on the way to being fitted for a pair of concrete boots, but I'll make sure I call you before they throw me in the harbor."

"You better. I'll want to know exactly how it happened and whether they're as scary as they look in the movies."

I frowned. "And of course you'll trace my phone so you can call the police and tell them where I am, so they can come save me."

There was a pause, in which I was sure she was shrugging. "Depends on how good you are with your description."

I laughed and shook my head. "All that aside, it's still not what's currently going on."

I leaned on the counter and looked at Mirror Katie again, mentally discussing the current situation with her instead. She looked great. I'd give her that much. Her chestnut curls had gone through a bout with a curling iron and were more controlled tonight, and she was wearing a new red dress, which hugged all the right curves, and a red lip.

She even had red heels on.

She looked like she was going out for a hot date. Which was exactly what she was doing.

"So what is it?" Lindsey finally asked. "What's so important that you needed to call me on a Friday night to get more advice? I should really start charging you by the hour."

"Charge me by the hour and I'll charge you for the updates I give you on my account," I said. "I know you're living vicariously through my brushes with crime. I know how lost you'd be without those updates."

There was silence on the other end of the line, which meant my threat had hit home.

"Okay, go," she grumbled. "What do you need?"

"I think I've made a mistake. I agreed to have dinner with Adam tonight. At a restaurant."

"... But it's Friday night," Lindsey said slowly. "Is this a... date?"

"It's not supposed to be," I said, half miserable and half excited. "At least I don't think it's supposed to be. But is it?"

"Well, dinner on a Friday night doesn't say casual, if you ask me," Lindsey noted. "Did he label it?"

He hadn't. He'd just said that he wanted to meet up and talk about the case. We were having more and more trouble finding times to meet that didn't seem totally suspicious if anyone was watching us, and we figured we may as well just make it obvious that we were becoming friends—at least, that was the story—so we could get a solid hour or two in for a meeting.

The fact that it was on a Friday night, and at the best, most expensive restaurant in Houston had become a complication, though.

I leaned forward and put on another coat of red lipstick, trying to remember what I'd heard about how to keep it on through a meal. Maybe that didn't matter, though. Maybe I'd just use that as an excuse to leave dinner if it got too weird, or if we had one of those moments where things got entirely too charged and we spent too much time staring at each other.

"It's just a business meeting," I told her, making my voice sound firm and sure of itself. "It's nothing more than that. Just so happens to be on a Friday night. At the nicest restaurant in Houston."

"Well, the nicest restaurant makes sense," Lindsey said quickly. "I mean, he's like a billionaire. He doesn't exactly want to eat at the diner on the corner."

God bless her. That was a good point, and something I hadn't even considered.

"And it gives us a chance to get a solid two or three hours together," I added. "It's getting harder and harder to sneak that sort of time. So this gives us a chance to actually talk."

"Well, there you go," she said. "Sounds like you've already got it all figured out. I don't even know why you needed to call me."

"To hear someone else say it," I admitted.

"Katie, you're good," she said, all conviction. "This is business. He wants to hear about the case. That's it. And I doubt it's a problem that you're probably looking freaking gorgeous. Any man would count himself lucky to go out to dinner with you. Just go there, report what you've got to report, and get back out. Don't pause. Do not pass Go. Do not collect $200. And definitely don't sleep with him. Get the case finished and get home."

I nodded, eying Mirror Katie and seeing that she agreed as well.

Get there, give him the information, and get back. No problem. When she put it that way, I didn't even know why I'd been worrying so much.

This was going to be easy. And bonus: I'd bought a brand-new dress and new shoes, and put them on Adam's company's account. This was, after all, still part of the contract.

⸻ ❧ ⸻

"YOU," HE SAID AS I sat down, "look freaking amazing."

I grinned in pleasure. "Thanks. I never thought red was my color, but this dress is starting to change my mind."

"I'm not sure the color would matter," he murmured, his eyes dancing down my body and then back up again. Then he jerked his head a bit, seeming to realize what he was doing, and brought his eyes back to mine. "Drink?"

"Wine," I said, my skin warming where his gaze had touched it. "Red."

He motioned for the waiter—who, I noticed, appeared almost by magic, courtesy, I was sure, of the enormous tip he thought he'd get—and quickly ordered a bottle of their best red. Then he turned back to me, his face wearing a very professional, very serious mask.

It was a mask that looked very, very good on him.

76

"So," he said, "now that I have you alone, let's get down to business. What do you have for me? Anything new?"

Ah. The unfortunate part of the night.

"Not yet," I admitted. "I've been through every inch of Charles' records and I can't find anything else that he might be lying about. There are those college transcripts, but I can't figure out why he lied about them, and I can't figure out whether those lies mean he's doing anything else."

"What about his spending account?" Adam asked quickly, his mind moving through the information almost as fast as mine.

I pointed at him in confirmation of his coming to the same conclusion as I had. "Now that's where things get kind of weird. He used a whole different password for his spending account. And I've been into a lot of other people's records. No one else did that. It's not company policy to have separate passwords like that."

A frown crossed his face. "Well, that seems suspicious. Is he hiding something?"

"Don't know yet. I had to go through all the options I had on my list, and then combine some of them to get in. I didn't get in until yesterday and I haven't had a chance to go through much yet."

This was the point at which I expected him to give me some trouble. Because this meant that I was lagging behind the deadline I'd set for myself. It shouldn't have taken me this long to get into those additional records, and it definitely shouldn't have taken me this long to go through them.

If I had hired me, I would have accused me of slacking.

I wasn't. I knew how quickly we needed to get through this case, not only to stop Adam's company from losing any more money, but also so I could get out of this situation and get home, where it was safe and I could live a life free of hot, sexy billionaires that I had to avoid to keep myself out of trouble.

And those things were foremost in my mind. I wanted to get this case over with.

I'm serious. I hadn't been delaying because the thought of going home and not getting to see him anymore felt like a pit opening up in my stomach. I hadn't been procrastinating because I wanted to have one more week of seeing him in the lobby of the hotel and the halls of the building where we worked.

I definitely hadn't been stalling because I liked the way his eyes lit up when we saw each other by mistake.

I just hadn't had time to go through the records yet. That was my story, and I was sticking to it.

To my surprise, though, he didn't give me any trouble for not getting through that stuff yet. Instead, he grinned.

"Well, I don't know how you haven't gotten through them yet, Katie. I mean, it's not like you're in a new job and trying to fit in, so probably doing twice as much work as you should be or anything."

I laughed and nodded. "Something like that. Same for you?"

"The opposite, actually. I did that for the first few days, but then I realized that I was attracting way too much attention by being too good at the job. The supervisor didn't believe that I was just some sales guy who happened to really love his job. I guess I was looking too much like a CEO who wanted the company to make money."

He looked abashed at the description, and that made me laugh even more. I took a sip of the wine—which was amazing—and glanced down at the label.

"Oh my goodness," I muttered.

Because I recognized that label. It was a wine I'd never have been able to afford on my own. A wine that I'd always wanted to try and had never been able to stomach the idea that it cost $500 for a single bottle.

"What's wrong?" he asked. "Is the wine bad?"

He quickly poured a glass for himself and took a gulp of the wine... then cringed, making a truly hilarious face.

I looked at him, shocked. "What," I asked, "is with the face?"

He put the glass down like it contained rocket fuel instead of $500 wine. "That tastes *horrible*."

I took another sip, actually paying attention this time. But the wine was... delicious. I mean, maybe not $500-a-bottle good, but very good.

"It tastes like a really nice shiraz," I told him, confused. "Oaky and full of boysenberries. Should go very nicely with heavy meals like Italian food and steak."

He just looked at me like I might actually be trying to teach him nuclear physics. And in that moment, I realized that I had a wine virgin on my hands.

"Are you... a wine virgin?" I gasped.

He narrowed his eyes at me. "I am not any sort of virgin, thank you very much," he snorted.

I narrowed my eyes right back. "But you don't drink wine, do you? You don't know the difference between a shiraz and a rosé. And I bet you have no idea whether you like merlot or not."

He pressed his lips together and took a deep breath through his nose, like he was actually offended that I'd guessed his secret. Then, quite suddenly, his face relaxed, and he tipped his head back and forth, rolling his eyes. "What can I say? I haven't exactly been friends with the sort of people who drink it. And my parents..."

Oh, now I wanted to know everything about how and why he'd never tried wine.

I lifted my glass and took another slow swallow, then pushed his wine glass toward him again.

"The secret," I said, "is how you drink it. Don't gulp. Pick up the glass, smell the wine to get a feel for it, and then take a small sip. And start talking. What about your parents?"

———⬤———

THREE HOURS LATER, we had barely talked again about the case, but I knew that his parents hadn't had much money and had therefore never had fancy things like wine in the house, and even when he was old enough to drink, he'd been too busy to drink anything that took time, like wine.

He'd also never tried the best restaurants in New York. Or rather... Well, he'd eaten there. But he'd never slowed down enough to really savor the food. He'd always been in a meeting or on his way to a meeting, and had completely skipped the part about actually appreciating the food.

"I demand that you go back to them and take your time," I said simply. "There's too much good food in New York for you to miss out on it."

He tipped his wine glass—full of his third pour—toward mine and clinked the glasses together. "I'll do that. And I'll insist that you come with me to make sure I slow down and savor it."

I stared at him, the wine buzzing in my veins and my breath growing still in my lungs, and knew that I'd had way too much to drink to answer that invitation. He'd had too much to drink if he was even offering it. He knew we couldn't do anything with the electricity arcing between us.

I knew it, too.

And that was why I bit my lip as I stared at him, letting my mind run right through the idea of kissing him, finally figuring out what he tasted like and sampling it. And when I ran my tongue along my bottom lip, I saw his eyes go down to it and then come back up to mine, and something happened deep in my stomach.

I arched my back and felt the answering tingle between my legs, and felt my lips part.

Shit, what was I doing? I'd had way too much wine to even be sitting here with this man. Wine that made me willing to play dangerous games.

I should get back to my room. Immediately.

"Want to get out of here?" he asked hoarsely.

"Absolutely," I answered.

The problem, I realized a second later, was that I didn't know exactly what he meant by getting out of there.

⟫●⟪

"SO, HERE WE ARE," I murmured, coming to a stop in front of my door. "Thanks for dinner."

"Thanks for coming," he said. "Sorry we didn't get to talk much about... Well, what we were supposed to talk about."

I turned to him and let my mouth curve in a smile. "You mean that whole case we're working on?"

He nodded slowly, and I fought to keep my smile from getting even bigger.

The man could not hold his wine. He might not be completely drunk, but he'd definitely lost the edge that usually made him sharp and a little bit overwhelming, like he was taking up more room than he was supposed to.

"What're you smiling at?" he asked softly, his gaze dropping down to my lips.

"Nothing," I lied, my voice breaking a bit as I leaned back, trying to get some distance between us.

Instead of letting me go, though, he leaned forward, propping his hands on the wall on either side of my head to cage me in.

"Nothing?" he asked, raising one eyebrow in an expression that was pure sex.

My entire body lit on fire. "Nothing," I breathed, already knowing exactly where this was heading, and doing nothing to stop it.

Instead of saying anything else, he moved toward me, his lips coming down over mine in something that was both demand and question, need and want and hot and wet and mind-numbingly bone melting.

I gasped and opened my mouth, tilting my head to invite him in, and his tongue swept into my mouth, starting a dance with my own as he stepped forward to press me against the wall, his hands going right into my hair and grasping it like he wanted to use it to control me. I arched my back off the wall and pressed against him, taking in the hard body up against mine, the hard length of him pushing against my stomach and telling me exactly how much he wanted me.

Hot damn, the man was a freaking giant. Taller than I'd ever realized and so broad that he could have picked me up with no problem, and the idea got me even hotter. I wrapped my hands in his shirt and pulled him even closer, needing more of him. Needing to feel him harder against me, hotter and bigger and—

His hands slipped down to my ass, pulling me against his hard cock as he deepened the kiss, and I groaned aloud, my hips starting to rock with need.

This was too much. It was too much. And some part of my mind—a part that I hadn't been listening to up to this point—was screeching at me, telling me that this was a bad idea.

A bad, bad idea.

Because this was the man who had hired me to solve his case. This was my client.

This was the man I had told myself I absolutely, definitely would not mess with while we were on the case, because it would affect my reputation and my ability to finish the case.

I jerked away, gasping, and stared at him for a long moment, trying to get my pulse to go back to normal and my brain to start working the way it was supposed to.

"I have to go to bed," I mumbled. "Early morning tomorrow, you know? Thanks for dinner. I've got to go."

I turned and fled into my room without even pausing to see how he reacted.

My mind was already trying to come up with ways to fix the enormous mess I'd just made of our professional relationship.

CHAPTER 12

ADAM

I WOKE UP WITH RAGGED breath, a fine sheen of sweat across my skin and my cock already in my hand, rock hard and aching with the need for release.

I quickly let go of it, sat up, and grabbed for my phone.

It was 7 in the morning on Monday, and this was the third day in a row I'd woken up hard and aching for Katie. It was also the third day since I'd talked to the woman in question. Because since that hot kiss in the hall—the one we'd both known we shouldn't take part in—she'd been avoiding my calls.

She'd also, I suspected, been hiding in her room and living on room service. I hadn't been able to spot her in the halls or the lobby of the hotel, no matter how much I tried, and when I'd gone past her room, thinking that I might knock and make sure she was okay, I'd found a 'Do Not Disturb' sign on her door.

I hadn't knocked.

The truth was, I still didn't really know how to interpret what had happened between us. That kiss had been hotter than any kiss I'd ever shared with any other woman, and I'd never had a woman avoid me after kissing her.

Hell, I'd never kissed a woman like that and then had her actually run away from me the way Katie had.

I knew I wasn't supposed to be messing with her. I knew we had a case going on, and that it was more important to solve that. But on Friday night, the wine had made it seem like an okay idea to kiss her.

I mean, more than an okay idea. My entire body had been screaming for it. Demanding that I run my fingers through her hair and pull her to me, seal my mouth over hers and make her mine. When the opportunity had presented itself, I hadn't thought twice about it.

Hell, I hadn't thought once about it. I'd just done it.

And she'd responded, arching her back and melting into me like she'd been waiting for me to do exactly what I was doing.

And then she'd jerked away from me and run into her room.

I gasped in pleasure at the memory, and looked down and realized that I was rubbing my cock, my body already reacting to what we'd started on Friday night.

Fuck, I had to get up and get to work. I had a thief to catch and a mystery to solve. I didn't have time to lie around in bed, dreaming about Katie and how soft and pliant and sexy she'd felt when I had her pressed against the wall, her hands wrapped in my shirt and my cock throbbing with need.

I jerked myself up out of bed and made my way to the bathroom, trying desperately to get my mind to focus on the problems at the office, rather than the way Katie had opened her mouth and invited me in when I kissed her.

⸺◉⸺

"CHARLES RAY, AM I RIGHT?" I asked the tall, gangly man in the break room. He was doing something with the coffee maker and whirled around, surprised, at my voice.

He wasn't a memorable fellow, I registered quickly. Pretty generic in terms of look. Taller than most, but not so much that it would have made him stand out in a crowd.

He was exactly the kind of man who would go unnoticed. The kind of man that no one would point out as a criminal. I wondered if that was how he was getting away with it.

I wondered if he counted on himself to look just like everyone else, so that no one was suspicious of him.

He grinned when he saw me, but I could see that the grin was sort of wavering on the edges.

Something had him on edge. Keeping secrets would do that to a person, I guessed.

"Adam, right?" he said. "One of the new guys from corporate. I met one of the girls who came in with you the other day, too. She said corporate had been keeping resumes in case they needed to plug some holes in the satellite offices."

"Right, that's exactly it," I said, commending Katie on her quick thinking. It was a part of the story that we hadn't gone over, but her

84

reasoning made perfect sense. "I guess we must have been at the top of the list."

"From what I've seen, they sent the best," he said, his gaze sliding to the side. "James says you're blowing our sales figures out of the water."

And now his tone had turned... suspicious. Jealous, even. Like we were somehow in competition.

What in the name of tech was going on here?

I shrugged. "Just doing my job. I've been studying sales and marketing since I was in college, so it's a good fit, I guess."

"I guess," he replied.

And that was it. He brushed past me without saying anything else and stalked down the hall like I'd said something to offend him.

I watched him go, completely confused at the entire exchange. What the hell was that?

And if that guy was doing something wrong, shouldn't he be doing his best to act normal rather than acting like he was actually hiding something? Acting like he was made it even more likely that he'd be caught.

I headed back to my cubicle, already planning what I was going to tell Katie when I called her. Because that man was definitely hiding something.

And I had a very strong suspicion that it had to do with padding his expense account—and not wanting anyone new coming in and figuring him out.

<hr>

"OLIVER, PLEASE TELL me you've got something for me," I said sharply, my cell phone held to my ear as I walked out of the office and hailed a cab.

"Wish I could, boss, but the truth is, the guy's got nothing on him. He passed all the checks they did when he was hired, all his references checked out, and he's had a clean record since he arrived. I think you've got the wrong guy."

I pressed my lips together, displeased at this. I didn't want to have the wrong guy. I wanted to have already found the person responsible. I wanted to wrap this case up before it got any worse.

"And there's more," Oliver said, interrupting my thoughts.

"Oh shit, what now?"

"More money has gone missing," Oliver said. "In the same way. Nothing overt, nothing super obvious. The accounting department picked it up in one of their audits."

I groaned. "How much more?"

"Another $3 million."

Wait. That was... odd.

"All at once? In one chunk?"

Because if someone was stealing $3 million at a time, that was a whole lot different than just lifting off some of their accounts. That was more than just padding expenses.

That was outright theft.

"Impossible to tell," Oliver replied. "They can only see that the money isn't matching up where it should, and that's the amount we're off by. But they don't have any idea where it's gone, or when, or how. I'm telling you everything I know."

"Shit," I breathed.

I'd wanted to find the guy—or girl—responsible for this, before it was too late. Before things got even worse. And it looked like 'worse' was already coming to pass.

"What does Katie think?" Oliver asked suddenly, his voice changing to the sly tone he used when he was interested in a woman.

"Katie," I said sternly, "is working on it. She's mining information as quickly as she can, but if there's nothing to find on that guy, it means we're barking up the wrong tree."

"She barking up *your* tree yet?" he asked, his tone even more suggestive than his words.

And for some reason, it set me off. Oliver and I had been friends for years, before we even started working together, and he'd teased me about countless women. He'd seen me with one-night stands and serious girlfriends, and he'd even talked me out of getting engaged once.

I had never, not once, taken it personally when he teased me about a girl.

But hearing Katie's name in his mouth, knowing that right now he was probably drawing a picture of her n his head—even though he'd never seen her—made me want to walk right to the nearest wall and punch a hole in it. It brought every single possessive cell in my body to bear, and had all my hair standing on end, ready for a fight.

What the hell was going on with me?

Then he made it even worse.

"She hot?" he asked. "Or is she one of those cops who looks more man than woman?"

"She's an incredibly talented PI, Oliver, and that's all that matters," I said stiffly.

I heard him snort and knew he didn't believe me. But that was all he was going to get from me. As far as I was concerned, this conversation was already over.

"Look, I have to go. If Charles Ray isn't the guy, it means Katie and I have to adjust our route. Especially if more money is already missing. I'll call you if we have anything,"

I hung up before he could answer, still annoyed with him—for some reason—for asking about Katie, and was already dialing her number by the time I got into the cab.

CHAPTER 13

KATIE

I WENT TO WORK THAT morning still thinking about the phone call I'd received from Adam yesterday. The one where he'd sounded annoyed and almost... not frantic, precisely, but something a whole lot like it.

Like someone had gotten right under his skin and he'd immediately called me to make himself feel better about it.

Or something.

Honestly, the thought had warmed me right down to my soft, gooey center, and I'd gone through what I had on Charles Ray with him—for about the third time—and then gotten off the phone smiling for reasons I didn't truly understand. I mean, the man had hired me to look into this case for him and find out what was going on. It hadn't been surprising that he called me when he had new information on our prime suspect—and on more missing money. I would have been annoyed with him if he hadn't called.

Calling me had been the only logical step.

So why the hell had it made me feel like he was handing me some sort of secret, hidden part of himself? Why had it felt like he was telling me about more than just the case we were working on together?

And why in the green fields of Texas was that glow still with me when I woke up this morning, lasting all the way through my shower and a hurried breakfast, to accompany right into the cab that was going to take me to the office?

Probably, a voice in my head told me, *for the same reason that you spent the entire walk through the reception area looking for him, and are already wondering if you'll see him in the lobby at the office.*

Well, shit. Said voice was right. I was just hoping my snarky inner demon would have missed out on the part where I was way too excited to see him, even in passing, and felt a secret thrill whenever I saw his name on my caller ID. Because I was doing *my* best to ignore that little problem.

Seemed to me that the voice could do the same, if it knew what was good for it, or had any love for me at all.

Still, considering how often that voice came around to tell me things I didn't want to hear, I was probably giving it too much credit, thinking that it actually cared what I felt on matters like this.

———⬤———

I GOT TO THE OFFICE still awash with that stupid glow, which I couldn't quite bring myself to wish away, and got through the somewhat foggy, moist morning and into the lobby of the building with a sigh of relief.

Then I started looking for Adam. I hadn't seen him since our dinner, and I hadn't talked to him much either, aside from his somewhat panicky phone call, and to my surprise, I was sort of... well, missing the sight of him, if I was being honest. Missing that crooked smile he liked to wear, and the cocky tilt he always had to his shoulders. The confidence in his walk, which he always cut down as soon as he realized that anyone might notice it.

The way he'd never had Midori sours or wine, but had taken my word for them being good and ended up having way too much.

The heat of his body when he pressed me up against the closest wall and made me wish we weren't in public. The way his mouth had felt on mine, and the roughness of his fingertips on my skin.

I bit my lip despite myself at the thought, and then remembered—courtesy of someone running right into me—that I was in the lobby of Miller and Co, and as such, should really not be thinking about stripping Adam Miller completely naked and letting him have his way with me.

Also, I was working for the man. I really had to do better about keeping that in mind. I was a professional, and I was here to do a job. A job that would never go well if I let go of my self-discipline and slept with him. Or even told him that I wanted to.

I straightened my shoulders, lifted my chin, and put my very best professional mask back on, making sure that it covered all the holes I had in my mental mask as well. Find where the money was going, get the job done, and go home. Find where the money was going, get the job done, and go home.

89

That was my mantra from now on. And that was all there was to it.

Of course, at that moment, I let my gaze rake across the lobby... and found Adam on the other side of the room, watching me.

He cocked his head, a confused look on his face that told me that he'd definitely seen the mental argument I was having with myself. And then he grinned and gestured toward the elevators. Was I going up? Did I want to ride together?

Unfortunately, getting into an elevator with the man who had my blood singing in my veins was probably the worst idea in the history of ideas.

I shook my head and gestured vaguely for the bathrooms—an idea that would send any man running, thank goodness—and Adam nodded quickly and turned toward the elevators himself.

Though I did watch him long enough to see him throw another glance over his shoulder at me. I smiled and gave him a little finger wiggle, intended to send him on his way, and then waited for him to disappear into the elevators. The moment he did, I walked to the elevator bank myself and pushed the button again.

Because I was going up. I just didn't want to do it in the same car as him.

⸻ ◉ ⸻

TEN MINUTES LATER, I was strolling through the lobby of my department.

"Morning, Andrea," I said to the girl who functioned as our receptionist.

She looked up from filing her nails—something she seemed to do every second of every day—and gave me a bright smile. "Morning, Katie! You here to do some genius number crunching today?"

I rolled my eyes theatrically at her. "Another super exciting day of adding millions of numbers together, because what else could I possibly be doing with my time?"

She tittered happily and went back to her nails, and I reminded myself once again to talk to my boss about getting a receptionist who was even slightly interested in what our department did. I was positive Andrea was great at answering phones and forwarding calls,

90

but if the department ever needed someone to stand in for a sick employee, the receptionist would be a great place to pull from.

Only if that receptionist, however, had any interest in handling more than her nails.

Hey, I was at Miller to help Adam figure out who was stealing money from him. There was no rule that said I couldn't help him with some other inefficiencies at the same time.

And speaking of inefficiencies, the moment I got through the door and into our actual department, my supervisor, Jan, practically tackled me.

"Katie, thank goodness you're here."

I looked at her, somewhat concerned by this opening. "Why? Is everything okay?"

"I have an account that I can't make heads or tails of," she said, her voice hushed like this was some big secret. "Can you come take a look?"

I nodded and following her, still wondering what all the drama was about. When I saw the paperwork, though, I could see why she was so confused. We were looking at the spending account for Charles Ray—something that I'd just barely managed to get into, even with all my hacking experience—and the numbers were most definitely off. I took the stack of paper back to my desk, looking at it as I walked, and saw that there were a number of inconsistencies.

Namely, the expenditures didn't match the list of prices from the vendors he was working with.

The expenditures weren't larger, though, which was what I would have expected from this particular person—who was, after all, our prime suspect. If he'd been padding his expenses, making it look like he was spending more money on supplies than he actually was, I wouldn't have been surprised.

In fact, that had been exactly what I'd been expecting to see.

But this was the opposite. Instead, the amounts he was spending were... less than the amounts the vendors should have been charging.

What in my Uncle Bob's beard was going on here?

———◆———

THE FIRST THING I DID when I got back to the hotel was head for Adam's room. I didn't call or text first, mostly because I'd seen him

91

arrive right before me knew for a fact that he was already in the hotel.

Besides, the things I needed to tell him—like that Charles Ray was looking less and less likely as our suspect—couldn't wait. I didn't want him to waste any more time going over employment records for the guy if he wasn't *our* guy. Charles Ray was doing something, all right, but I couldn't find anything that looked like stealing.

At the moment, it looked a lot more like he was actually getting better deals with the vendors than anyone else.

We needed to move on to a new suspect.

I knocked sharply on the door of Adam's room, looking down at the papers I'd brought with me and trying to make sure that I was seeing what I thought I was seeing.

When the door swung open, I looked up, my mouth already open to start talking.

I snapped it shut when I saw Adam standing in nothing but a towel.

Holy hell, his abs—and his pecs, and his arms—were just as impressive as Lindsey had said they would be.

"Oh shit, I'm sorry," I said, immediately turning away. "I didn't expect to catch you in..." I gestured toward him, not even knowing what to call his current state of undress.

"In a towel?" he joked. "I don't blame you. It's not exactly my usual uniform. I was just about to get into the shower, though. Do you need something?"

He didn't sound like he was mad. He didn't sound anything but friendly.

But I suddenly couldn't get that kiss in the hallway out of my head. I couldn't stop thinking about the way he'd felt, and the way I was already arching my back, enjoying the heat between my legs, told me quite clearly that my body hadn't forgotten it, either.

"Katie?" he asked, his voice quieter now. "Are you okay?"

I looked up at him, knowing full well that my heart was showing all over my face, and forced myself to nod. "Fine," I said quickly. "It's just that I found some new information today and I wanted to come bring it to you right away because I think we're looking at the wrong guy and we need to find another suspect and—"

He yanked me into his room, slammed the door shut behind me, and had his lips on mine before I could finish the run-on sentence I'd started.

And heaven help me, I liked it. I liked it way too much.

I pressed into him, lifting my chin to kiss him harder while I threaded my fingers through his hair, pulling his head down harder against mine. He backed me up several steps toward what turned out to be a table, and pushed me to a sitting position, spreading my legs so he could stand between them, and holy fucking hell was he hard. I gasped as his cock nudged against my leg—while cursing the tightness of the skirt I'd decided to wear—and settled for kissing him harder, our tongues dancing and our teeth clashing together.

Adam broke the kiss and put his lips to my neck, leaving a hot, wet trail on my skin from my jawline to the top of my blouse, and I gasped, throwing my head back and daring him to go further.

Fuck, I wanted the man. Every single cell in my body was screaming for him.

But the moment he reached down and started to inch the hem of my skirt up my legs, I realized what we were doing.

And reality came crashing down on me with all the subtlety of a one-ton boulder.

"Shit, we can't do this," I gasped.

Because we couldn't. For so many reasons that I couldn't remember right now, but would write down later, when my brain was in control of my body again.

I reached down and pushed his hands away, then pushed him back, very carefully not looking down at where his towel was wrapped around his nether regions. I stood up, straightened my skirt and my blouse, fought the battle of a lifetime to get my face back under control, and looked up at him, forcing myself to be cool. Calm. Collected.

A numbers nerd, not a woman raging with fire for the man standing in front of her.

"You know we can't do this," I told him calmly. "Way too many complications. For your company. And my reputation."

He nodded jerkily, and I could see him fighting his own battles in his mind.

Luckily, logic was winning out.

"You're absolutely right," he rasped. "I'm sorry. I don't know what I was thinking."

I let out a breath of relief at his agreement. "Probably the same thing I was," I said, my gaze going to his lips and then jumping back up to his eyes. "We weren't. I've got to go, but I wanted to drop these off. I've got lots of notes there to explain what it all means. We have to find a new suspect, Adam. I don't think this is our guy."

I got out of the room without saying anything else. Mostly because I didn't trust myself for one more second with Adam Miller and his towel-clad and extremely hard body.

CHAPTER 14

ADAM

AFTER ANOTHER NIGHT of—you guessed it—barely sleeping because I couldn't get my mind off of the woman I'd hired to try to solve the problem that I should actually be more concerned with, I headed to the office early.

Hey, I'd always been the kind of person who thought that if you couldn't sleep and you weren't doing anything useful at home, you were probably better off being in the office getting work done. This might not be my office, and I might not be calling the shots for the entire company's future here in Houston, but the same held true.

I still had work to do. And I could still do it better in the office than I could at home, where my suite was now doing an obnoxiously good job of reminding me of Katie. How she'd looked at that door. How she'd looked when I pulled her in.

The way she'd felt with her legs wrapped around me, kissing me like her very life depended on it.

I groaned, throwing my head back against the seat of the cab and trying to decide whether it was better to remember it or try to put it out of my mind.

She'd taken about three seconds to get the hell away from me and hadn't made any secret about the fact that she didn't think it was a good idea for us to be taking part in activities like that.

I mean, she was right. I knew she was right—and I'd known it while it was going on. We were professional allies, and she was a woman I'd hired. We both had reputations on the line. We had a case we were trying to finish.

Neither of us could afford to let ourselves get sidetracked. Or put our professional resumes at risk.

Which was exactly why I walked into the lobby of the building without even thinking about Katie Walters or whether I would see her there. I didn't glance around the lobby looking for her chestnut curls or those curves that she dressed so well. I definitely didn't look for those glasses or the red lipstick or the energy she seemed to carry around with her.

When I saw her right in front of me, though, leaning on the counter of the coffee cart and laughing with the barista, my blood froze in my veins, and I stopped in my tracks, incapable of going one step further.

When she turned around and saw me, her eyes going wide and dark, her lips pressing into a sudden pout, I knew she'd done the same thing I had this morning. She hadn't slept well, and she'd gotten to the office early in the hope of distracting herself from the very thing that had kept her from sleeping.

Namely, me.

I bit my lip, trying to figure out whether it was safe to go over to her or not. I knew I wanted to—my whole body was screaming for it—but I wasn't sure it was a good idea. Hell, I wasn't even sure it was a *safe* idea. And in any other life, in my office in New York or some anonymous place, I would have thrown caution to the wind and strolled right up to her, a cocky smile on my lips and my shoulders set with the confidence that I felt whenever I was around women.

But this wasn't my office, and it wasn't an anonymous space. It was the Houston office. A place where my supervisor was already too close to recognizing me, and a place where I absolutely didn't want to be caught. Getting caught here would mean tipping off whoever was stealing from me. It would mean giving that person a chance to get away with it—and even continue it.

I couldn't afford it. I'd been through this before, and I knew it to be true.

And that meant I couldn't afford to do one single thing that might draw more attention to me. I definitely couldn't do anything that might tip anyone off to my real identity.

And that was why I gave her a slight smile and a shrug, and then turned and headed for the elevators instead of the coffee cart. I wanted to go talk to her. I didn't know if I'd ever wanted anything more—aside from my company, which had consumed my entire adult life. But I simply couldn't afford it. On a number of levels.

Going to the elevators, getting to my own floor, and going to work was the safer option. It was the more responsible option. And I was sure she would have told me that except same thing if I'd asked her.

So I didn't feel guilty about doing it.

I didn't regret it at all.

Seriously.

———◉———

BY BREAK, I HAD ALMOST completely talked myself into agreeing with that decision. I'd been on the phone all morning and had done more deals today than I'd done all last week. Yes, I knew I wasn't supposed to be standing out, and I'd told Katie that I was going to cut down on the number of sales I did, just to keep from making James any more suspicious than he already was.

But when it came to a choice between selling the hell out of my clients today and finding Katie and literally dragging her into a closet and forcing her to tell me how she felt about me and what we were going to do about it, the sales were the better option.

I was sure of it.

Still, when I got up for my break and made my way toward the break room, my mind, free now of work and client relationships, went immediately back to Katie and how she'd looked with her legs spread out on that table.

And damn, was it difficult to keep walking with my cock getting hard so suddenly.

I changed my route before I got to the hallway that held the break room and headed in a completely different direction, thinking that I didn't want to run into anyone in the break room in this shape. Maybe if I walked through the department, I'd manage to get myself under control.

Think of something else, I told myself. *Anything else. Numbers. Think of numbers. Those aren't sexy. They're the opposite of sexy.*

Unfortunately, they were also Katie's specialty, and the thing she talked about almost all the time.

So numbers were out.

Dammit.

Chemistry. Think of chemistry. Totally not sexy.

Chemistry like what I had with Katie?

Shit.

97

I was used to my brain being at my beck and call, and almost always doing exactly what I wanted it to. I wasn't okay with it going off on tangents like this. Acting against my wishes. I wondered if this was what it felt like to be crazy, with voices talking to you and such. Your mind doing things you didn't agree with.

Fuck, I was going insane over the PI I'd hired to figure out who was stealing money from my company.

I rounded a corner, my focus on my brain rather than what was in front of me, and ran right into someone.

I went stumbling back, shocked, and immediately started apologizing—at the exact same time that Katie Walters turned around and started apologizing to me.

We both stopped and stood completely still, staring at each other with our mouths hanging open.

Finally, I found my voice. "What are you doing up here?" I asked, my voice coming out a whole lot hoarser than it should have.

"My... my supervisor asked me to bring up some paperwork," she said faintly.

She looked at me for a long, tense moment, and then she seemed to melt and give up some sort of fight she was having with herself.

"Fuck it. That's a lie," she said. "I came up here because I wanted to see you. Not... not to talk, exactly, but because... because..."

I took three steps forward, took her by the shoulders, and brought her up against my body, pressing my lips against hers before she could finish her stumbling statement. And to my surprise, she kissed me back, sealing her body to my own and opening her mouth for me, her hands going to the front of my shirt and tangling in it like this was exactly what she'd come for.

I took a second to appreciate the feel of her against me again, and another to be surprised that she was letting me kiss her. Then I saw a closet behind her and reached out and grabbed the doorknob.

When the door opened without any resistance whatsoever, I pushed her right into it and followed her, my lips still sealed to hers, my hands already itching to get her clothes off and feel her bare skin under my fingertips.

⸺⸺◦⸺⸺

THIS WAS A BAD IDEA. It was a bad, bad idea.

And I didn't give one single fuck. I gave less than one single fuck. I gave a *negative* fuck.

This woman was everything. She was incredibly gorgeous and even smarter than she was beautiful. She was tough and hard-working and clever, and she'd started her own company from scratch and made it successful. She'd stood up to what I knew was a male-dominated industry and become the best in the business.

She was my match in every way. And I had never met a woman who made my blood run hotter than her.

She was also a wildcat in my arms right now, biting and scratching and clawing as she tried to get at me, her kisses hot and passionate, her breathing telling me exactly what she wanted. Not that I would have had any question. Her body was lithe and ready, pressing against me in a language that every adult knows. The language that said she was hot and ready and wanted nothing more than for me to slide into her and make her mine.

I tore my mouth away from hers and dropped it toward her ear, taking the lobe in my teeth and nipping her slightly.

She gasped, just on the edge of a moan, and her hips rocked against mine, her body pressing against my throbbing cock.

I almost moaned in response. Then I remembered we were in a janitor's closet at the freaking office.

I clapped my hand down over her mouth and looked her calmly in the eyes, shaking my head and putting one finger up to my lips. We had to be careful, or we were going to get caught. And neither of us could afford that.

Her eyes got wide and even darker with need, and she nodded once in acknowledgement.

Then I ducked in and started kissing her again, my hands going to the hem of her skirt and pulling it quickly up to her waist. Which was when I realized that she hadn't worn any panties.

I broke away from the kiss and gasped, a fresh surge of lust rushing through my body.

"Dammit woman," I hissed. This was almost too much. I'd already known the girl was sexy, but coming to work without panties on...

Then I got my brain to start working again. And it presented me with some problems.

"Are you sure?" I asked, breathing heavily and praying she'd say yes.

She looked up and met my eyes with hers. "Absolutely."

She didn't have to tell me twice. I spread her legs and stepped between them, undoing my belt and pants and allowing them to drop to my ankles. It wasn't sexy. It wasn't sophisticated. And I didn't have time to wait. I reached down and slid my fingers between her legs, making her throw her head back in sudden bliss, her fist in her mouth.

And then I drew one of her legs up around my waist, positioned my cock so it was right up against her opening, and slid in, lifting her up so she would take it to the hilt the first time. I opened my mouth in a silent moan, reveling in her hot, wet body around me.

And then I started moving.

And hell, if I'd thought I knew anything about heaven before, I hadn't known one single thing. I actually slowed down, holding my breath and forcing myself to pay attention.

Because this woman.

I looked down at her and then ducked to kiss her, sliding my tongue into her mouth as I started moving again, and soon we were moving in tandem, our bodies dancing as our tongues played with each other, and the rest of the world—and the office right outside of that door—fell away from the world we were building together.

CHAPTER 15

KATIE

"LINDSEY—"

"Don't tell me. You need help."

I bit my lip and threw myself into the chair in my sitting air. "I don't know."

She paused. "You... don't know?"

And now came the tricky part. I'd just gotten home from the office, my entire body still buzzing with what Adam and I had done in that closet. I could still feel his fingers dancing across my skin, the phantom of his nails in the skin of my wrists as he held my hands above my head and drove into me, my legs twined around his waist and pulling him deeper and deeper until we both flew over the edge, our mouths open in silent screams, our bodies orgasming together between the mops and brooms of the janitor closet.

It had been the most intense experience of my life, and I didn't regret one moment of it. My body wanted to do it all again, right now. And then again in the shower. And then again when we got back in bed. I wanted Adam's arms around me, his lips on mine.

But could I tell Lindsey that? Was it wise to tell anyone? Because we had a whole lot to lose if people found out that we'd done what we just did.

And I just wasn't sure I was ready for that sort of risk.

Things I maybe should have thought about before I called her.

Then I realized that I would have called her anyhow. Because Lindsey was my best friend, and I'd just done something that I thought might cause me professional problems. I needed advice.

And there was no one I trusted more than Lindsey when it came to advice. Particularly when that advice was about men.

"I slept with him," I told her, going for the short, sweet version. There was absolutely no reason to try to make it pretty or fancy. The problem was clean and simple.

I'd done what I had promised myself I absolutely wasn't going to do.

Instead of going immediately to the fact that I'd told her I wasn't going to do that, though, Lindsey started shrieking.

"What?" she shrieked. "You what, you what, you what?"

I could practically imagine her jumping up and down, now, the jumps timed with the questions, and I smiled despite myself. No, it wasn't what I was expecting. But it also made me feel immediately better.

"Well, at least someone's excited about it," I said, grinning.

"You slept with him?" she asked—still shrieking.

"Damn woman, do you want all your neighbors to know?" I asked. "Can you please keep your voice down, at least a little bit? This isn't the stop-the-presses news you seem to think it is. And it's not exactly something I want everyone in the world to know about."

That seemed to bring her back down to earth, and I knew Linds well enough to know that she was doing some quick calculations, and remembering what I'd said about not wanting to put my reputation at risk. Because she might be a party girl, and she might have wanted me to get with Adam right from the start, but she was also responsible, in the right situations.

And she was more committed to me than anyone else had ever been in my life. She was there for me no matter what she was doing. If I'd told her that I didn't want to sleep with him because I was worried about what it would do to the company and to my career, she'd remember—and she'd be right here with advice for what to do now that I'd broken my own word and given in to the man who had hired me.

"Okay, first question: Where were you? Second question: How was it?"

I sighed, wondering how many of the details she expected... and then I jumped right into the story, giving her all the details I could manage, because nothing less was going to do. I wanted her to know exactly what had happened—and how I'd felt about it.

I mean, how else was she going to give me advice for how to deal with it?

It wasn't like I wanted to relive the entire thing, blow by blow, and remember exactly how it had all felt.

Though I wasn't going to complain about that.

By the time I was done, Lindsey's voice was so tense with excitement that I expected her to start shrieking again at any moment. I was surprised when she was still serious when she started talking again.

"Do you think anyone heard you?"

"Shit, I hope not. Though I don't think so. Adam made sure I knew that we had to be quiet. He has even more to lose than I do."

"Well, even if they did, it's not like this is your real job," she retorted.

"Oh, you mean the job where Adam Miller hired me to help him figure out what was going on in this office and why it was costing him so much money?" I asked. "You mean that job?"

She giggled. "Given the story you've just told me, I don't think you have to worry about getting fired from that one, Katie."

I frowned. "I don't want to keep my jobs by sleeping with the men who hire me, Lindsey."

"Honestly, I don't think he would have fired you even if you didn't," she said quickly. "You're too good at your job. And if you ask me, he knows it. Why else would he have hired you?"

I thought about that for a moment. It was a good point, and I decided I was going to take it and make it mine. Believe in it wholeheartedly.

Because I agreed with her. After that encounter in the closet, there was no way Adam was going to fire me.

Though that didn't mean it could happen again.

I was going to have to make sure it didn't. No matter how much my senses were screaming for it.

CHAPTER 16

ADAM

"I'M TELLING YOU, I think we have a problem with him," Katie was saying breathlessly. "I was at my desk and he came and stared at me for thirty seconds, then moved on like nothing had happened."

I frowned. She'd busted into my room right after work, breathless and definitely freaked out, and though I thought at first that she was going to talk about what we'd done in the closet—which would have made sense as the reason she was freaking out—she had instead started talking about Charles Ray.

She'd been at her desk, and he'd come right up to her and stared at her like he knew something about her but hadn't asked any questions or said anything. He'd just walked away.

I'd thought I was officially supposed to be suspicious of him for business reasons—and I definitely was—but I was also starting to feel like he might be a danger to Katie herself. And that was rubbing me all sorts of wrong.

"We've got to make a move on him," I said without thinking twice about it. "It's got to be him. Why else would he be acting so weird? Just because new people came into the office? That's no reason to act like you've definitely done something wrong."

"Well, we don't have any proof that he has," she pointed out.

We did, though. "We have those faked college transcripts," I said quickly.

She shook her head, though. "Those don't mean he's stealing money. They mean he maybe shouldn't have been hired, or that the HR department down here—and even the sales department—should have done better research before they hired him. They should have done their freaking jobs. But that seems to be a problem that quite a few people have down here."

That one caught my attention. "What?"

She huffed, but flipped her hand like it was something we'd talk about later. "Some of their processes aren't what they should be, and definitely aren't efficient, and I've got some thoughts about their personnel. Don't worry, I've got it all written down. It'll be in the report I turn in when we finish this contract."

"*If* we finish this contract," I said darkly. "Because Charles Ray and his behavior aren't our only problem."

She frowned. "What's wrong? Did something happen?" She moved like she was going to take my hand or get closer to me, and I froze, waiting for just that.

It wasn't necessary, of course. Nothing was wrong. Nothing had happened that would require her to comfort me. But the idea that she was going to—that she felt comfortable enough to try to take care of me—made my heart beat three times as hard as it had been.

Which, of course, was ridiculous. This was a woman I had literally hired to take care of me. The idea that she was trying to do so now was nothing short of expected. It was part of her freaking job. We were here talking about the mission itself, and I'd made it sound like something was wrong.

Of course she was going to try to take care of me. It was in the contract we'd signed.

There was nothing more to it than that.

And that should have been all I needed to know. I should have been able to just take that as the truth and put the whole thing behind me. Stomp down on that feeling of a balloon being in my heart and stretching bigger and bigger until it was about to pop.

Get my freaking emotions under control.

It had never been a problem before. I'd been around plenty of women, and I'd never felt like I was losing control in the past. Hell, I was generally a cool customer when it came to dating. I could date a woman and keep my emotions removed from the situation, and pick them back up again after the relationship was over.

So why the hell was this random PI, recommended to me by a friend and here only because I was paying her, causing this reaction in my body?

"Adam?" she asked softly, a frown creasing her brow. "Is everything okay?'

Oh. Right. We were in the middle of a conversation, and I'd just told her that Charles Ray wasn't our only problem.

Dammit, I needed to get my head in the game. I was lucky I wasn't trying to make any large CEO-type decisions, with how distracted I'd suddenly become.

"It's okay for now. I think," I said, answering her question. "But I think we're going to have a problem, at some point. The guy who supervises sales, James Andrews, is getting suspicious. He already said that he recognized me the first day I was there, and he keeps bringing it up. I think I've given him a pretty good excuse, but it's making me edgy as hell. And he's also going on and on about how many sales I've pulled off in the short time we've been here."

"I thought you were going to cool it on those," she said, sounding like she might actually be teasing me.

I made a face. "I was. And then a certain someone came to my hotel room and saw me in a towel and turned around and ran the other way, and I got a little bit distracted. I needed something to take my mind off that certain someone. I chose selling my ass off the next day as the best route. So that whole not-drawing-attention-to-myself thing..."

"Didn't work so well," she said, skipping right over her role in the situation and nodding wisely. "Right. So we've got to do something about your sales. And your face." She glanced at the face in question, her lips twitching with laughter. "Though I'm not sure how we can disguise you at this point. Everyone already knows you." Then her smile fell away. "Wait, are you sure you haven't met him? At some sort of event for execs or something? Could it be that he actually recognizes you from something you two did together?"

I shook my head quickly, because I'd been through every memory I could bring up, and knew for a fact that I'd never met the guy. "We don't usually have events that include supervisors and execs in the same space," I said, realizing as I was saying it that it sounded incredibly stuck up. "Not because there's anything wrong with the supervisors. It's just that there are so many of them."

She held up her hand in a 'stop' motion. "Believe me, I get it. Supervisors live in an entirely different world than execs. It wouldn't make sense to mix them. But how else could he recognize you?'

"The employee handbook, most likely," I said, cringing. "They have my picture front and center as CEO. And it'd be on the wall of every break room in every building, in case people bothered to look.

We have our execs there to 'motivate' people." I did the air quote where they belonged, hating that I was even saying this.

She looked like she was going to start laughing at any moment. "To motivate people? That's... special."

"It wasn't my idea," I said, my tone void of any emotion. "I think it's just as stupid as you do."

She burst out laughing and put her hands over her mouth. "Oh, thank goodness," she said when she stopped. "I was afraid to say anything, but shit, that's conceited."

"I know," I moaned. "And I'm afraid he's seen my picture and that it's going to blow our cover. We could be found out just because someone in the HR department in New York thought my face would help other people work harder."

She put a single finger to her lips in a classic thinking pose and frowned, letting her brain work on the problem. "Then I guess we only have one choice," she said solemnly.

"What?" I asked. "And please don't say plastic surgery. I sort of like my face the way it is."

She reached across the table we were sitting and brushed her fingers across the back of my hand. "I sort of like your face the way it is too. So not plastic surgery."

My heart jumped—at the contact, at her admitting that she liked my face, and at the thought that plastic surgery wasn't actually on the table.

Then I told myself to grow the fuck up. What was this, seventh grade, that I was getting so excited about hearing that a girl liked me?

I realized very quickly that I didn't have to be in seventh grade to get excited about that sort of thing, and then immediately put the whole argument away. We had much bigger fish to fry right now. Fish by the name of Charles Ray and James Andrews.

"We have to close this case as quickly as possible," she said finally. "It's the only way to guarantee that we get out of here before you're found out or we get in some other sort of trouble."

I didn't ask what the other sort of trouble might be. I thought I probably already knew. And I was more interested in how she thought we were going to close this case as quickly as possible, when she'd just told me, in this same conversation, that our main suspect couldn't actually be the guy we were looking for."

"And what," I asked, "do you plan to do to get this case closed? Because I'm pretty sure you told me just a few minutes ago that Charles Ray couldn't possibly be the guy."

She pointed right at me, as if that was the entire point.

"But you said that it's weird that he's acting the way he is if he's *not* the guy, and I think you're right. He's been entirely too sneaky about things to be completely aboveboard. He's got to be hiding something. And he's doing other weird things, too. Like getting his goods for less than he should be."

"Wait, what?" I hadn't heard about this, yet, though I vaguely remembered her shoving papers at me and saying something about the prices not matching up.

I thought that was the same night that the towel thing had happened. Which explained why my memory was a bit foggy.

She went through the numbers she and her boss had found, quickly outlining how Charles' numbers had been off, and in the wrong direction.

"So... that doesn't seem like stealing," I pointed out, speaking slowly like this might not have occurred to her.

She made a face at me. "Of course not. It's the opposite of stealing. But if you've stolen $3 million and you think you're about to get caught..."

I slapped a palm to my forehead. "You try to put the money back so you can point out that it's right there, and ask the people doing the catching what they're talking about," I concluded. "Oh my goodness, you're right. Maybe he's already onto us and is trying to cover his butt."

"Or get the jump on us," she agreed. "We need to know what he's doing in his personal time, though. Whether he's made any big expenditures or has an account with a bank that only handles large transactions."

I nodded. "Smart. Small banks aren't exactly built to hold millions of dollars in deposits. But how are we supposed to find out what he does on his free time?"

She reached out and tapped me once on the nose. "Easy. We go to his house this weekend and stake it out. Follow him when he leaves. See where he goes and whether it's of any help to us. Are you in?"

I just stared at her, too surprised at first to come up with an answer. I'd known I was hiring a PI. I hadn't thought that would mean we'd be going on actual stakeouts.

CHAPTER 17

KATIE

THE NEXT DAY, THE FIRST thing I did when I got into the office was seek out Charles Ray himself and try to get a feel for him.

Okay, the second thing.

Look, I'd always been really good at feeling what people were like. I'd been a good judge of character since the day I was born... or at least the day I started being able to remember such things. And judge people. I'd always known whether people were lying to me or not, through some miraculous sixth sense that I'd never bothered to look too closely at.

That sense, though, was the thing that had encouraged me to become a private investigator. Yeah, my uncle's death had been the driver, but my sense for whether people were telling the truth or not was the thing that had made me think I might actually be really good at it. It had certainly worked when it came to the guy who killed my uncle.

And I was hoping it would work as well today. Charles had acted sort of edgy the first time I talked to him, and he'd been even edgier—and definitely creepy—when he just showed up in my cube, stared at me for a long moment, and then turned around and left without even saying anything to me about, you know, whether he needed anything or not.

At that point, I'd been so paranoid that people were starting to figure out that Adam and I were more than just two people staying in the same hotel that I hadn't gone after him. I'd wanted a plan for what I was going to say when and if he asked.

Well, now I had that plan. And I was going straight to his cubicle to try to get a read on what, exactly, he was lying about. Because Adam's supervisor and our little jaunt into the janitor's closet had both moved our timeline up by a lot.

I wanted this case done before it cost Adam's company any more money, and before anyone decided to unmask us.

I was also definitely making a new rule for the company. If I was going undercover on a job, I was refusing to take anyone else with me. Especially if they were ruggedly good-looking, incredibly charming, and way too sexy clients who would definitely get in the way and provide temptation that I didn't want to deal with.

I stopped by my desk first so I could drop off my bag and gather a pen and pad, and then I made right for the sales department, calling a sort of vague greeting out to my supervisor as I passed her office.

I didn't want her asking any questions about why I was going to sales when I'd literally just arrived. My official story was that I'd been working on Charles' accounts since Jan had first asked me to have a look at that paperwork that didn't make sense, and that I'd found something else I wanted to talk to him about. Sure, I could have emailed him, but that probably would have taken longer than actually going to his desk, where I could ask questions and we could work the problem out together in real time.

I was trusting that story to be enough. If anyone asked for more detail, I was going to have to make it up on the fly. But this early in the morning, before anyone had had much coffee?

I was betting no one would really care about the details of the problem.

In fact, I was banking on it.

I got through the lobby of our floor without anyone even approaching me, and when I got on the elevator, I had it to myself. *Score one and two for Katie,* I thought, smiling slightly. A quick ride had me on the sales floor, where I also found very few people at their desks.

"Ghost town this morning," I said to myself.

Then I bit my lip. Shit, what if Charles wasn't even in yet? This office didn't seem to have any real structure when it came to the workday, counting on people to do their eight hours at some point within a given window, and though I already knew what time Charles generally started, courtesy of having access to all of his records, I hadn't even thought to check that he was here already this morning.

Well, if he wasn't, I was just going to have to make this entire walk again later and hope for the same good luck when it came to no one else approaching me. Because this was a conversation that needed to take place as quickly as possible. I was done with fooling around on this case.

I wanted answers, and I wanted them now.

When I got to the cubicle marked with his name, though, he wasn't there. A quick glance told me that his chair was still neatly pushed in, his computer not yet on. The pens he kept in a cup on the desk were still all in said cup, and I didn't see any briefcase or sign of a travel mug.

Dammit. Of all the days for him to decide to get here late.

I strolled through the walkways between the cubicles, though, thinking that he might have stopped to talk to someone else. And when I got to the break room, I found him. He still had his briefcase with him and was here pouring himself some coffee before he even went to his desk.

Which was... Well, honestly, it wasn't weird at all. It just wasn't the way I did things. That didn't make it suspicious. I was just reaching.

"Morning, Charles," I said, walking in and putting on my best and brightest smile. "You're exactly the man I was looking for! Glad to have found you. Have you had enough coffee to go over some numbers with me?"

He turned around, cast one panicked look at my face, and started stuttering.

"Oh, new girl. Hi. Um, actually, I don't have any time right now. I have a... meeting. Yeah, a meeting. Should be starting any minute. I just wanted to get some coffee before I sat down, you know? Sorry, I have to run. Maybe we can chat later."

He actually pushed me out of the way in his hurry to get through the door and back out into the hallway, and by the time I regained my balance and went to follow him, he'd disappeared.

Now, logic would have said that it was pointless on his part, since I knew where his cube was and could quite easily follow him. But I was betting that if I did go to his cube, I'd find it still empty.

I was also betting that there was no meeting.

And that he'd made right for the men's bathroom, counting on me not to follow him.

"Right," I murmured to myself. "A meeting. Hm."

I walked out of the break room and made my way back toward the elevator banks, my phone already out and a text to Adam taking form in my mind. I didn't think we had enough to finger Charles as our thief. But he was definitely hiding something, and I was becoming more and more convinced that we needed to figure out what it was. Maybe finding that would lead us right to the information we needed to figure out whether he was the one stealing money or not.

———◦———

BY THE TIME I GOT BACK up to finance, the department had come alive again. It was like everyone had suddenly appeared the moment I stepped into the elevator, and the department had come whirring to life, the worker bees getting to their positions and starting their daily grinds.

I walked into the office to find the place absolutely humming with activity.

It was such a change from the office I'd left fifteen minutes ago that I stopped for a moment, trying to get my bearings—and gave Rachel just enough time to find me.

"Oh. My—" she gasped. "I saw that guy, Adam, downstairs on his way into the building and he actually held the door open for me and offered to get me a coffee. That man is so fucking hot. I'm so jealous that you're sharing a hotel with him."

I chuckled, though I felt a bit of a knot form in my stomach at the mention of Adam. And the idea of him buying coffee for Rachel.

"Well, it's not like we're sharing the hotel, really. We don't have the entire place to ourselves," I said. "Though that would be something, wouldn't it? Five floors for him and five for me."

"Unless you chose to share the floors," she said, batting her eyes to make her meaning perfectly clear. "I know I would share my floors with him any day of the week. And twice on Sundays."

"Oh fuck," I groaned. "He's good-looking, but I'm not sure he's that good-looking." Then, realizing that I had the perfect person at my fingertips, given Rachel's obvious tendency to gossip—and know about everyone in the office—I changed subjects. "Hey, Rachel, do you know Charles Ray, who works down in sales?"

She made a face. "Sure do. Why?"

I held up a hand to stop her right there. "Hold the phone. What's with the face?"

113

She made another face at me, this time even sassier, and then grinned. "*You* hold the phone. Who even says that anymore? Like... cops from the '70s?"

"I obviously say that," I said drily. "Now tell me what you know about him that led to that face."

Another face, and this time it was sort of resigned. Like she was about to tell a story she didn't really have time for. Which, I thought, was rich, when it was going to be coming from the biggest gossip in this entire company. I couldn't imagine a story Rachel *didn't* want to tell.

Maybe it was just so boring that she didn't like it. Actually, that sounded like it would definitely be a story she wouldn't want to tell. It just wasn't the one I wanted to hear.

"And don't leave out details just because you think they're boring," I added, thinking I'd better get the jump on her there.

"Oh my... Fine. Though I don't know why you want to know about him. He's nothing special. I mean he's really boring."

She cringed at that, and I almost laughed. It was just such a childish thing to say, though she acted like being boring was roughly the equivalent of being completely pointless. Though maybe, I thought, in her world, that was true. She was hands-down the most outgoing person I'd ever met, aside from Lindsey, and 'boring' might well be her idea of the End of Times.

In which case, I guessed, I was no one to judge her for it.

"He might be boring, but he's also got some wonky accounts," I told her firmly. "Spill it."

She rolled her eyes. "Okay, well I don't know that much about him, so you're bound to be disappointed. He's been weird since day one. Doesn't make friends in the office, doesn't come out with us for drinks. I don't even think he goes to the Christmas party, honestly. Total lone wolf, only calling him a wolf is being way too kind. More like lone crane or something, with how tall he is. Keeps to himself, acts like everyone is out to get him. Acts like he's hiding a secret, but what kind of secret could a man like that actually be hiding?"

Suddenly her face turned sly and suggestive.

"Not like that Adam. He looks like he has all kinds of secrets. The kinds that would get a girl into the best sort of trouble. Has he told you any of them yet? You know, quiet little conversations in the elevator at the hotel?"

She smiled and gave me a coquettish look, ready for any details I'd managed to come up with on the new boy in school.

I just sighed. Yeah, I knew his secrets. And no, I wasn't going to share them.

Though I had a feeling that one secret in particular—which had happened in a janitor's closet on the sales floor yesterday—would get Rachel to shut her mouth and stop looking at him the way she was.

That thought felt way too possessive of a guy I hardly knew, though, so I grabbed it and shoved it back into the closet it had come from, telling it firmly to stay put and let me do my job.

If not even Rachel knew anything about Charles, then my hunch was right. We were going to have to go on an old-fashioned stakeout to see whether it told us anything more about the guy. Which meant Adam and I were going to be spending a whole lot of time in a car together. This weekend.

CHAPTER 18

ADAM

I STARTED ASKING PEOPLE about Charles and what they knew about him as soon as I got into the office, the feeling that Katie and I had both been sort of dropping the ball heavy in my stomach.

We'd come all the way down here and done this whole undercover thing just to catch this guy. And then we'd gotten here and gotten sidetracked.

Now I wasn't saying we'd been sidetracked by each other, specifically... but I also wasn't saying we hadn't been. And I knew that in my case, specifically, I'd been dragging my feet because I was dreading the thought of going back to New York and not seeing her every day.

Yeah, that was really contradictory, considering I needed to figure out what was going on in this branch so I could get it stopped, and doing that required both Katie and me to do our jobs and get things sorted out. Get the case finished so we could get it fixed.

Still. I was man enough to admit that I hadn't been pushing as hard as I could have been. I was also man enough to say that it needed to change. Something told me we were running out of time, and I just wasn't willing to head back to the city without getting this thing sorted out.

Unfortunately, no one else seemed to know any more about Charles than we did. Hell, given the blank stares I was getting from some of the people in the department, they'd never even heard the man's name. I was surprised at this, given the supposed family atmosphere of this particular branch, and the fact that the sales department wasn't big enough for people not to know each other. There weren't exactly hundreds of employees on this floor. More like fifty, max.

A big enough number that *some* people might not know of Charles Ray. But everyone?

By the time break rolled around, I'd collected exactly zero information on the guy and returned to my desk, thinking that I made a pretty rotten private investigator. Though at least this particular morning's investigation had kept me from selling anything, which would help me in my new mission not to stand out to my boss.

I was just getting into the first client file, trying to sort out what they might need and how I might offer it, when that very boss appeared in the doorway of my cube.

"Adam?" he asked, his voice sounding tense and sort of awkward.

I spun around in my chair. "James, what's up?"

He looked down at his feet. "Um, do you have a second so we can have a short meeting in my office?"

Well, shit. When you're trying to fly under the radar and not get caught masquerading as nothing more than a simple employee, and you're actually the boss of the entire joint, the last thing you want to hear is that the guy in charge of supervising you—who already thinks he recognizes you, and hasn't realized yet that he definitely does—wants to see you in his office.

"Um, actually I'm kind of in the middle of this file," I said, making it up as I went. "I've got some really good ideas to get this client to make a pretty big purchase from us and I'd like to jump on it right away rather than waiting. Can we do it later?"

James shook his head, looking like he wanted to say yes, it could definitely wait until later, but didn't have that choice. "I'm afraid not," he said. "The work is going to have to wait for a second. Don't worry; I'm sure that sale will still be there later."

Shit, shit, and double shit. This was getting worse by the moment. Still, it wasn't like I could still tell the guy no. I'd just used the one and only excuse that might get me out of this meeting.

A meeting that James obviously didn't want to have. Something that was making him nervous as hell.

Shit, they'd figured out who I was, I realized. Something or someone had blown my cover, and now they were going to ask what the hell I was doing here and why, and the whole thing was going to be a wash. Plus it would be all over the company's gossip network. Everyone would know that I'd come down to Houston to run an undercover mission with a—

Wait, had they found out about Katie, too? Because if not, then she'd be able to stay here and keep working on the case.

If they didn't know about her, I thought, I wasn't going to give her up.

And then I realized that I sounded like I was about to become a prisoner of war, laughed at myself, and got up to follow James to his office, where I would be facing the music. Whatever happened happened. I'd deal with the outcome the same way I'd dealt with everything else in my life: by owning it and figuring out where to go from there.

I was really surprised when I got to his office and found that there weren't any other supervisors or execs in the place. I'd expected the heads of this office to be in attendance to break the news that they'd figured out who I was and now needed to know exactly what I was doing.

I cocked my head, wondering if I had it all wrong. Could it be that James didn't know who I was, or what I was doing here? Had he actually believed my excuse for why he probably recognized me?

The man in question closed the door behind me, though, and that made me immediately wonder, again. Maybe he was breaking this news to me on his own, and didn't want anyone else involved. That seemed like it would be a weird call, but hey. Weirder things had happened.

So I was even more surprised when, instead of saying something about how he'd figured out where he knew me from and wanted to be in on the whole scheme, he handed me a card. I looked down at it, confused, and slipped it open to see a $100 gift card inside. To a steakhouse.

"What's this?" I asked, truly wondering what it was. I mean, I obviously knew it was a gift card. "Or should I say... Why's this?"

I glanced back up at him, trying to figure out what the hell was going on here. What was this, a bribe of some sort?

Was he trying to bribe me with a $100 gift card to Tom's Steakhouse? Because that... would be weird.

"It's a gift card," he said unnecessarily.

"Yeah, I got that part," I said, a smile starting to grow on my lips. "But why? Did I win a raffle I didn't even know I'd entered or something?"

He chuckled. "No, no. It's a thank you for all the hard work you're putting in. Hell, I could barely get you away from your desk, and I asked you personally! You're hands down the hardest worker I've ever had in this department, and the fact that you're so young and so new just makes it even better. I can see a bright future for you here, Adam. Working as hard as you do, you'll be running the company the next thing you know."

I almost choked, but caught it just in time and shoved the sound back down my throat.

"Um," I said instead. "Are you sure? I mean, I don't want to cause any problems here in the office or anything. You know, jealousy."

Dammit, my whole plan had been to fly under the radar. Evidently, though, I was complete shit at flying under the radar. Evidently I was the most radar-tastic person to ever radar.

He shook his head. "Everyone knows you're outselling everyone else, but we all like you too much to hate you for it," he told me quickly. "We all want to know your secret! You're almost too good at this job to be believable!"

And that right there was exactly what I was afraid of.

Excuses time.

"Well, I'm real, I can tell you that much. And my mother could tell you the same. She's been riding me for my entire life to be more fantastic at a whole range of things. As for my secret, I can't say I have one. Just love the job, I guess. Love the company, love the product. When you really believe in what you're selling, it makes it easier. But I'm sure everyone here already knows that."

I worked to inject humility and embarrassment into my voice, though the words were the truth. I believed in these products like they were my babies. Probably because they were.

"What college did you go to, if you don't mind me asking?" he asked.

When I told him, and admitted that I was an Ivy League snob, he snorted with laughter.

"We had bets running on it," he admitted. "And we thought one of the big colleges in California. You know, one of those UC schools. The ones that give you such good networking opportunities. We had you nailed as a big basketball fan who went to all the games and got straight As on the side."

Okay, now this was getting really weird. How much time had these people spent talking about me and dreaming up an entire life for me? I'd only been here a little over a week! And why in Hell's name were they all so interested?

I'd thought I might be drawing too much attention to myself before, but I'd thought it was constrained to James himself. Now I realized that the entire floor was evidently spying on me. They'd probably also tried to figure out who I was dating and what I did for fun.

I hoped like hell none of them had followed me back to the hotel and seen me hanging out with Katie. That wasn't something we'd reported to HR, though we were supposed to, and then finding out about us would be incredibly inconvenient.

"I do actually like basketball," I told him warmly. "And my school had a really good team. But you're giving me too much credit with the grades. I was a mediocre student, at best."

Totally untrue. I'd aced every class. But I needed to sound like I wasn't the golden boy they were making me out to be. I needed to make them think I was at least somewhat normal.

He just chuckled and shook his head. "Those grades obviously didn't say much about your promise, then. Keep up the good work, Adam. We're lucky to have you on the team."

He ushered me out of the office and sent me on my way, a brand spanking new gift card in hand, and I headed back toward my cube, feeling like everyone was watching me—because now I knew they were—and wondering whether I should grow this beard out even more to try to hide my face.

Shit, I'd already known I was drawing too much attention, but I'd never realized it was this bad. We needed to get to the bottom of this case *now*. Before I got caught and sent back to New York in disgrace.

CHAPTER 19

KATIE

"ARE YOU READY FOR THIS?" I asked Adam, looking doubtfully at what he was wearing. "We're not breaking into the house, you know. You don't have to..."

I gestured vaguely up and down his body, not thinking that I needed to say anything else.

Because the man was dressed completely in black. He was also wearing black boots and an honest-to-goodness black beanie.

He looked down at his ensemble as well, frowning. "What? I wanted to be able to blend in with the background."

"No one," I told him carefully, "blends in when they're dressed in all black. You look like you're trying out for an emo band. Or going to a Halloween party where you didn't want to get dressed up. We're just going to be sitting in the car. Not trying to blend with the darkness of the night."

I said the last sentence with a lower, more echoey voice, and he grinned appreciatively.

"So you're saying I could get out of these jeans, which are way too tight, and put on something more comfortable."

"I'm not just saying it. I'm recommending it," I confirmed. "You change. I'm going to run to the market across the street and get snacks."

"Snacks?" he asked blankly.

Shit, it was like this was the first stakeout this guy had ever been involved in.

Wait. It probably *was* the first stakeout this guy had ever been involved in. He was a CEO, not a cop or private detective.

"Yep," I said quickly. "We're going to be in that car for a while. We want to make sure we have things to keep us occupied, and things to eat while we wait. Unless you were just planning on fasting the entire time."

Now he finally caught onto the joke and lifted one eyebrow in an incredibly sexy move. "This body does not survive well without food."

"Exactly my point," I told him. "You change. I'm going to buy snacks. Do you have a particular fetish?"

The suddenly hooded eyes on them man in front of me told me that it had been the wrong choice of words. The flooding of heating through my belly and into my legs told me that I didn't regret it. We hadn't talked about what had happened in that closet yet, and I was thinking we were definitely going to have to. Soon. There was just too much tension between us to leave it be.

But we also had a long stretch of time in a car ahead of us. It could wait until we were there.

As fun as it sounded to have that conversation when we were trapped in a small space together.

"Food fetishes," I told him firmly. "Do you have anything you particularly want?"

"Fritos," he said quickly. "At least three bags of them."

Well, I hadn't seen that coming. The man had rock-hard abs and arms as wide as my thighs. I hadn't thought junk food would be on the menu. Still, I wasn't going to judge. Personally, I was going to bring at least ten cans of Pringles.

"You've got it," I said. "Change. I'll be back in a little."

<hr>

"THIS," ADAM SAID SHARPLY, "is boring."

He stuck another Frito into his mouth and chewed slowly, watching the house in front of us.

I turned and looked at it as well. He was right. It was boring. Mostly because it was nighttime and literally nothing was going on.

I mean, it was night. He was probably asleep. And now that I was coming around to that conclusion, it occurred to me that it might not have been the best idea to start the stakeout at night. Sure, if we'd been watching someone who was actually involved with the mob, like Lindsey wanted everyone to be, or who was running drugs or something, then watching them at night would have been logical. But Charles, if he was doing anything, was involved in white-collar crime.

Something that generally happened during the day.

Still. I'd thought when I was coming up with this plan that a night-time stakeout would be a good idea just so we weren't discovered. And that part was still true.

I was also starting to get really tired, though. And I was tired of Pringles.

"I have to admit, I'm starting to think that coming here for a night watch was a bad idea," I told him. "Though it seemed like a good idea at the time."

To my surprise, I felt a finger run up my arm, the touch light and tickling.

"Night's good for other things too, you know," he said quietly.

I turned to him, shaking my head. "We can't afford to take any time off from watching. That would defeat the purpose of the stakeout. What if he does something while we're distracted? It would mean we came out here for no reason!"

He looked at me like I'd gone crazy. "Katie, so far, he's taken out his trash, and now all the lights in his house are off. I'm guessing he went to sleep, like normal people do at night, and that we'll see him again in the morning. If we're still crazy enough to be here."

"We just have to be patient," I said primly.

Though honestly, I was starting to get pretty distracted by his fingers on my arm. And that distraction was leading to me actually considering the other stuff he was talking about.

Before I could continue my argument, Adam leaned forward, those light fingertips growing more forceful, and pulled me into a kiss.

It was so possessive, so hot, so unbearably sexy, that for a moment I just melted into it, my lips parting and my tongue inviting his right in. I gasped into his mouth, part surprise and part lust, and pressed back, my body reacting instinctively to his demand.

Then I realized what we were doing. And where we were. And who we were supposed to be. And I yanked back.

"We can't," I said quickly. "We're on a public street, for shit's sake, and we're supposed to be watching the guy we're investigating for stealing money from your company!"

Yes, I knew we'd also already had sex—in a closet at the office. And I knew that we'd been fighting the sparks between us since the first night we meant. But we hadn't even talked about that sex in the closet yet, or what it might mean, and here he was trying to start something again.

It was confusing. It was trouble. And great cinnamon toast was it hot.

I stared at him, knowing my eyes were big and my lips parted on what could have been a groan of need. And I was staring at him when his eyes cut to the clock and noted the time... and then came back to mine.

"It's after midnight," he murmured. "And we're in a neighborhood where everyone goes to bed by 10. We're also in an SUV with plenty of room and tinted windows. Come here."

It wasn't a question. It wasn't a request. It was a command.

And damn, did my body react to it. Heat rushed through my stomach and into my core, my legs going weak at that demand, and the expectation that I was just going to obey him.

Was this how he got people to do things in his office? Did he just expect that they'd do whatever he told them to?

Shouldn't I be offended that he thought he could boss me around like that? *I should*, a part of my brain screamed. I should be shouting that it was arrogant and cocky and—

The last thought died as he reached out, grasped me around the waist, and pulled me from the driver's seat and right into his lap.

"I want you," he growled, pulling me down and demonstrating how much he wanted me. His cock was hard and twitching through the loose jeans he'd put on when he changed, and it rubbed through the thin layer of my yoga pants, catching at my core and making me gasp.

"Adam," I whispered. "We can't do this. We haven't even—"

His lips interrupted me, crushing to mine and taking control of the situation, and I gave up and kissed him back, rocking my hips and rubbing up against the bulge in his pants, knowing that he could feel my heat moving up and down him.

I wished I'd had the presence of mind to wear a skirt. On a stakeout. Where I hadn't been intending to do anything with this man.

His hands slid down my back and under the waistband of my pants, pulling me down harder on him, and I broke the kiss and threw my head back, gasping. It was too good. The friction, the heat, the size of him.

The memory of how it felt to take him inside me.

"Backseat," he muttered. "I want to spend hours making out with you but I don't think I have the patience."

I didn't have to do much in terms of getting to the backseat, since he picked me up again and lifted me through the space between the two seats. Within moments, I found myself on the bench of the backseat, watching Adam clamber through the passenger door, yank open the door to the back, and climb in after me. He settled down on the seat and made quick work of stripping his jeans off.

I glanced down and caught my breath at the sight of him. I'd already thought the man was a Greek god, all hard muscles and smooth, taut skin, but his cock was something else entirely. It was standing at full attention now, hard and ready and bobbing.

Oh yes, this man wanted me. And given the slickness between my legs, my body was overruling my mind—which was screaming all sorts of reasons to be careful—and urging me to give in.

"Come here, Katie," he murmured. "I want you."

That note of command was back in his voice. And I wasn't in any position to tell him no.

I didn't *want* to tell him no.

I slid out of my yoga pants, my eyes on his the entire time, and watched his gaze turn hotter and hotter as I took my pants off.

"Your shirt, too," he said, his voice hoarse. "I want every inch of you."

I stripped out of my sweatshirt and down to my bra. "Yours, too," I told him. "After all, it's only fair."

He gave me a devilish grin and pulled his T-shirt over his head, leaving himself completely naked. "Come ride me, woman."

Damn, the man was bossy. And so unlike the more casual, relaxed man he'd been since we'd been working together. I didn't know what had changed, or why, but I liked it.

Heaven help me, I wasn't supposed to like a man ordering me around. But I did.

I climbed into his lap and hovered over his cock, my lower lip caught in my teeth. "What do you want?" I asked.

He grabbed my ass and pulled, but I resisted him.

"Katie. You know what I want," he groaned.

But now, I thought, it was my turn to be the boss. If only for a moment. Because we were both powerful players here, and that meant that neither of us could be completely in control of the other. I leaned forward and took his ear in my teeth, biting down slowly. "Tell me," I said.

He moaned quietly. "I want you, woman."

"Say please," I whispered. "And I'll think about it."

Instead of saying anything, he grabbed my hips and used his superior strength to pull me down on him, the length of his cock sliding into me up to the hilt, the tip hitting me in a place that made me want to scream with pleasure.

And I would have, except that his mouth had come down on mine, keeping me quiet while he started to move inside me.

CHAPTER 20

ADAM

WHEN I WOKE UP THE next morning, it was become the sun was coming over the horizon and shining right through the windshield and into my face.

I squinted against the light, my mind sputtering as it tried desperately to start up and remember where the hell I was that included sitting in a car with the sun shining right into my eyes.

Then I realized that I was also naked.

And then I realized that I also had a naked woman sitting in my lap.

I twitched, alarmed, and then looked down and recognized the tousled chocolate curls brushing against my face. Oh shit, it was *Katie*. What the hell was Katie—

Oh. *Oh.* Memory came flooding back, then, courtesy of the renewed blood flow to my brain, and I remembered it all. The stakeout. The car. The lights going out in the house we were watching, and Katie and I both growing bored.

Me kissing her, and her telling me we absolutely couldn't do that. Me pulling her into my lap and pointing out all the reasons that we not only could, but also definitely *should*. Her giving in a whole lot easier than I'd expected. And us crawling into the back seat, where she'd straddled me and ridden me until we both orgasmed so hard that I had to keep my mouth on hers to keep us both from screaming loud enough to wake the neighbors.

Damn, the woman was amazing. Smart and sexy and so clever, and so in-control, and so...

Well, so naked in my lap, my cock still buried inside of her, and hard again, courtesy of that morning magic.

I twitched, stopping myself from groaning at the last minute as I realized how tight and hot she was around me. I shouldn't, I thought. I couldn't. The woman was my employee, and she was also asleep. Regardless of what we'd done last night, and how hot she'd been in my arms, like a living flame, I knew I couldn't do what I wanted to right now.

But holy hell did I want to make love to her again. I wanted to grab her hips and start rocking her, reveling in the feel of her around me. I wanted to look up into her eyes and watch her as I made her dance for me again. I wanted to take her right to the edge and soar over it with her in my lap.

"Are you going to do something about that, or are you just going to keep sitting there?" a voice suddenly asked.

I smiled, spread my hands over her hips, and started to rock inside her, and moments later, her mouth came down over mine and started kissing me. Her hands tangled up in my hair and held me close, and this time, I thought, this time, I was going to take it slow. I wasn't going to let myself get in a rush and go through it too fast.

This time, I wanted to make sure it meant something. Because I was starting to think that this whole I Hired You as My PI might just be the start of the partnership we could create together.

⚬

"DONUTS," SHE SAID, shoving the box into the backseat and then crawling in after them. "They're a vital part of every stakeout."

She got seated and passed me a cup of coffee, and then took a sip from the cup she had in her other hand—and made a face.

"It's not terrific," she said apologetically. "But it's better than nothing."

I took a sip of the coffee and agreed with her about the not terrific part. It tasted like it had been on the burner for about five hours before it finally made its way into our cups. But she was definitely right about it being better than nothing.

And the caffeine was heavenly.

Suddenly, though, she reached out and grabbed me. "Duck!" she hissed.

We both hit the floor, our coffees notwithstanding, and I realized belatedly that we'd probably just lost whatever cleaning deposit we'd put down on this car. Not that it mattered.

I was more interested in why we were ducking.

"What's going on?" I hissed.

"Charles just came out of his house," she hissed. "Which you were supposed to be keeping an eye on while I was at the donut shop. Did you even bother to watch?"

"Of course I did!" I hissed back. "And if he just came out of the house, then it stands to reason that he was in there the whole time, anyhow."

She twisted her lips, unable to argue with this logic. Because she knew I was right. Instead of admitting it, though, she just narrowed her eyes at me, making me want to pull her into my lap and kiss that expression right off her face. Then she slowly rose up from the floor until she could see over the dashboard of the SUV.

"What's he doing?" I asked. "Something sinister? Holding up a sign that admits that he stole millions of dollars from my company?"

My blood heated at the thought, and I remembered why we were actually here. It wasn't so I could hang out in a car with a gorgeous woman, eating donuts. It was because someone from the Houston office had stolen millions of dollars from my company and was in the act of doing it again. I was here because I needed to find that person.

I was here because I was *going* to find that person.

And if it was Charles Ray, I was going to tear him limb from lanky limb to protect my company.

"Nothing so obvious," she said quietly. "He's getting into his car, though. Wait, he's going someplace. Quick!"

She scrambled through the opening between the front seats into the driver's seat, grabbed the keys from the center console and crammed them into the ignition, and took off down the road before I'd even gotten up off the floor. I'd started to, but the sudden action sent me sprawling back out on the carpeting, my shoulders getting stuck between the passenger seat and the seat I'd been sitting on last night when we...

Well.

I grunted in discomfort and got to work getting my shoulders unstuck.

"You could have warned me that we were going to start moving," I told her loudly.

She just snorted. "What, and wait for you to get into a seat so we could start? We'd have lost him, for sure."

"That," I said, breathing heavily as I hauled myself back into the seat, "is not the point."

"It's exactly the point," she said sharply, handling the truck like a pro as she maneuvered between the other cars on the road.

I looked ahead of us and saw the car that had been sitting in Charles' driveway. It wasn't sexy. Just a gray sedan of some sort. The faceless sort of car that people drive when they don't really like cars very much.

It was that faceless aspect that made me recognize it, actually. I'd seen it and thought that it matched him exactly.

Now it was absolutely flying through the traffic, ducking and weaving as it swerved around cars that were going too slow and flew around the bends in the road.

"What the hell is he in such a hurry for?" I asked, my adrenaline starting to pick up.

Because I wasn't going to say that he was driving like he was running away from us. He shouldn't even know that we were here, honestly speaking. But he definitely looked like he was either late for an important appointment or running from someone he didn't want to deal with.

That wasn't the way you drove when you were innocent. I didn't think.

"I have no idea," she answered from the front seat, her hands tight on the steering wheel. "But he's making it awfully hard to follow him while still remaining subtle about it."

She jerked the steering wheel to the left, went quickly around a car in our way, and then moved back into the lane we'd been in before.

"If he looks back here, it's going to be way too obvious that we're also flying through the traffic."

I leaned forward and propped my hands up on the center console so I could talk to her without shouting, feeling closer to her than I had any point up to today.

The truth was, this was the first time I'd felt like we were partners, actually working together rather than operating separately.

And I sort of liked it.

"Guess we'll just have to hope that he doesn't look back, then," I said. "If he's in that big a hurry and driving like that, I don't see how he could. He needs to keep his eyes on the road just to make sure he doesn't run into anything. He's not going to have time to look in his rearview mirror." I paused and watched him for a moment. "Though driving like that, he might want to keep an eye out for cops."

Katie huffed out a laugh, then pressed on the accelerator to make the light Charles had just sped through.

I didn't know where that guy was going, but it was obvious that she was intent on getting there right behind him.

⸻ ◉ ⸻

IT TURNED OUT THAT Charles was just going to a retirement home. He squeezed into the parking lot, literally slid into a parking spot, and jumped out of the car, running for the entrance.

Katie pulled into a parking space further from the entrance and we watched him, both of us probably wearing equally confused looks on our faces.

"This was what he drove like a bat out of hell to get to?" she asked, her voice mystified. "What, he has a specific window of time to get here?"

"And evidently doesn't believe in leaving the house on time for it," I agreed, annoyed and disappointed.

It might have been unreasonable of me, but I'd really been hoping he was doing something more interesting. Like driving to a meeting under a bridge, where he was going to slip an investor a briefcase full of cash.

Okay, maybe I'd been watching too many movies. But I was still disappointed.

The next stop—the barber shop—was nearly as disappointing, and after that he went to the market, then back home.

He didn't leave the house again.

We'd been sitting there for several hours, making sure, when Oliver called.

"I don't think it's Charles Ray," he said quickly.

"Huh?" I asked, finishing the soda that I'd had with my lunch. "Why not?"

Oliver jumped into a story that included an employee in New York who evidently took too much time off, and how Oliver thought it was weird. Personally, I didn't see much problem with them taking time off. All our employees got a full two weeks of vacation, and they were free to use it when they wanted. If they didn't have any left, they were docked pay.

It was a perfectly reasonable system.

"Oliver, they have time off so they can use it," I noted calmly. "There's no law against him doing just that."

"Still, I think you should look into him," he said, sounding annoyed.

"Fine, give me his name and information and I'll have Katie do a background check. Will that make you feel better?"

There was a short pause, and when he came back on the line, he sounded even more annoyed. "Katie? Why, because she's doing such a good job in Houston? Don't you think you should look into this yourself?"

I frowned, wondering at the tone. I'd never known Oliver to get aggressive. "Well, she's the PI I hired specifically to find out whether people in the company were doing anything wrong," I pointed out. "Seems like it'd be a waste to do something like that myself when I have someone who's an expert at it. Inefficient, you know?"

I swore I could hear him growl at me, though he'd obviously covered the receiver before he did it. When he came back on the phone, his voice was calmer.

"That makes sense. I just want you to catch this guy and put a stop to this."

"Probably not as much as I do," I pointed out. "Thanks for the tip. I'll let you know if she finds anything."

I hung up the phone and glanced at Katie, something still ringing wrong in my head. What had Oliver thought? That I'd just take his word for it and fire the guy he was talking about, because Oliver didn't like something about him?

Earlier this week, he'd been talking about wanting to get Katie into bed. And now suddenly he didn't want her doing her job?

That didn't make any sense at all.

CHAPTER 21

KATIE

I GOT BACK TO MY HOTEL room disappointed that the stakeout had turned out to be such a bust, but also completely positive that we'd had to at least try. Sure, he was looking more and more like he couldn't possibly be our guy, and my instincts were telling me that we needed to find someone new to focus on.

But. There was still something very off about him, and we weren't going to know what that was—or whether it was important—until we looked into him and tried to figure out what he was up to.

The fact was, he could have been doing anything over the weekend, and we needed to know whether it was illegal or not. The fact that he hadn't done anything really worth noting meant that we could (probably) officially cross him off the list. Turn him over to HR and let them worry about why he'd faked his college transcripts, how that had gotten through HR in the first place, and what they were going to do about it.

So all in all, not a loss.

Besides, getting us into that car together had led to something else: that hot moment in the backseat where he turned my world inside out and fallen asleep together afterward.

Is it just me, or does actually sleeping with someone—not having sex, but sleeping—do more to change your relationship than the sex part?

I'd never thought of it before, but there was absolutely no denying that we'd woken up, still tight against each other and with his cock still deep inside me, and something had changed. And it wasn't just that we'd started in on each other again, taking our time and really appreciating it.

It wasn't just that it had felt a whole lot more like something tender and beautiful between two people who really liked each other.

I mean, that was important, too, and I felt my skin starting to tingle just at the thought of it. But that wasn't all it was. After we woke up, we'd been... well, more partners than we had been before. It was the only way I could really describe it. Before, we'd been working on the same case, but we'd been doing it as individuals, each handling it in our own way and on our own time, more or less.

The moment we woke up—well, after that, honestly, because we took at least an hour to enjoy each other again—our relationship had been different. And it had carried on all day.

I wondered if that part was going to last.

I walked toward the desk in my room, dropped the overnight bag I'd taken with me, put the bag of uneaten Pringles cans down on the floor, and turned my laptop toward me. I had a name, address, and social that I needed to get down in my databases, to start searching. The guy Oliver had become suspicious of in the New York office.

Honestly, it didn't sound like he had much reason to be suspicious of him. From what Adam had told me afterward, he wasn't doing anything aside from using his time off. There was no crime in that.

He'd said that Oliver insisted, though, so I ran the info through my database, which looked up credit history, previous employment records, and any criminal history. Just to see.

There was nothing to see there. He was just a guy working a job who liked to take time off. Maybe had a video game addiction or just slept too much. Or maybe he had a girlfriend who lived out of town, and who he liked to visit.

"Weird," I murmured.

Weird that Oliver had insisted we look at him. Weird that Oliver had put him on Adam's radar when there was nothing there. Especially when Adam's accountants in New York had tracked the missing money down to account errors in Houston, not New York.

There was something there. My instincts were screaming about it. But I didn't know Oliver, and I didn't know his relationship with Adam. I knew some of his history and how long he'd been with the company. I knew that he and Adam had been friends forever, because Adam had told me as much.

I would have expected Oliver to play on Adam's team. So why did it feel like he was turning Adam right into a dead end?

I glanced at the clock, realized how late it already was, and made for the shower. It was only Saturday and I'd have all of tomorrow to try to figure out what Oliver was doing, and why. Right now, I wanted hot water, plenty of soap, and room service for dinner.

Then I was going to go to bed and dream about riding Adam in the back of a large SUV, his hands on my ass and his lips on mine as he filled me up and drove me wild.

———◉———

ON MONDAY, ADAM AND I split a cab to the office. It was safe enough, we decided. Everyone knew we were staying in the same hotel, and it didn't make one ounce of sense to each pay for a cab when we were going to the same place.

We split up in the lobby, though, as per our agreement to pretend not to actually be friends, and rode separate elevators to our separate floors. I could admit to myself that I felt more than a little bit of a twinge of disappointment when he left my side, because we'd spent so much time together over the weekend, and our relationship had shifted somehow.

It felt a whole lot like leaving your boyfriend after you've spent the entire weekend at his place. Not that I was calling Adam my boyfriend.

Not that I was thinking about spending the entire weekend at his place.

Because once we were in the office, I couldn't think about those things. I had to have my game face on and my eyes on the prize. Now that Charles was off our list of suspects, we had to find someone else. I needed to get back into the spending accounts and see who else might be missing money—or adding it back in.

I turned my mind toward that as I rode the elevator, trying to figure out the best way to track such things, and was still thinking about it, my brain only half on the world around me, when I stepped off the elevator and ran right into my supervisor.

"Oh, Katie," she said sharply. "Terrific. You're just who I was looking for."

I looked up, surprised and trying to force my brain back into focus.

"Katie?" she asked, staring at me like she'd been talking to me and I hadn't answered.

135

I shook my head sharply and gave her an apologetic grin. "Sorry," I said. "I was trying to figure out a more efficient way to search the spending accounts for discrepancies, and I lost track of the real world. You know how it goes. What's up?"

I expected her to laugh and nod at my statement, because surely everyone had done something like that at some point, but instead she just seemed to look down her nose at me.

Which was... weird. Why was she being so standoffish?

"The execs need to talk to you," she answered mysteriously. "This way, please."

I frowned, confused, but followed her back into the elevators and up to the executive floor. The floor Adam should have been on in this building, I thought with a bit of a grin.

You can imagine my surprise when I was shown into an office where Adam himself was sitting on the couch, his arms crossed and a frown on his face.

"Adam," I said, too surprised to remember that I wasn't supposed to know him well. "What are you doing here?"

"We have something we need to talk to you both about, actually," a man with gray hair and an expensive suit said from behind the one desk in the office.

I stared at him, and then ran my gaze around the room, taking in the others in attendance. There were me and Adam, obviously. Jan, my supervisor, and James, Adam's supervisor, were both there looking distinctly... either disapproving or uncomfortable. I couldn't quite tell which.

The man behind the desk looked annoyed. As did the other gray-haired gentleman, who had a sharp, frustrated look about him that branded him, in my mind, as a lawyer.

"What exactly is this about?" Adam asked, and I could see that he'd suddenly stopped being Random Sales Guy Adam and had become CEO Adam.

CEO Adam who was being called to the carpet by people who actually worked for him. And he was not pleased. Or amused.

The man with the gray hair—whose name I thought I should know—picked up a remote and hit a button, bringing a flat-screen TV down on one of the walls. Another click and a picture came up.

A black and white picture that looked like it was probably from a security camera. And a hallway that I already recognized. I glanced over at Adam and saw the same recognition on his face.

And I knew we were in trouble.

Within seconds, the screen showed me wandering into the hallway, my eyes on the papers I'd been carrying and my feet moving quickly. A split second later, Adam came around another corner and ran right into me. We spent what seemed a very short time talking. And then he had me against his body, his hands all over me and his lips on mine... and then we slid into the closet right behind us.

"Shit," I mouthed, feeling the curse in every part of my body and yet unwilling to say it out loud. I wanted to get up and storm out of the room, too angry at what I was seeing to bother staying in this meeting.

I didn't do any of that.

I didn't think it was a good idea to draw any attention to myself when the superiors had just caught me and another new employee sneaking into a closet. I just hoped there weren't any cameras actually inside the closet. Because if there were, and if they'd caught Adam slipping my skirt up around my waist and lifting one of my legs up so he could slam into me...

We were going to be in even bigger trouble.

"There aren't any cameras inside the closet, and I think we're all glad to hear that," Gray-haired Guy said, sounding smug. "But I don't think anyone here has any doubt about what went on in there."

Oh shit, I was actually going to die of embarrassment. I'd never thought it was possible before, but right now, in this moment, I was sure it actually was. My eyes flew to Adam's, and I saw him looking sternly at me, telling me to keep my mouth shut and let him do the talking.

Right. I was completely fine with that. Let him hash it out. That gave me time to figure out how I was going to protect my professional reputation if this got out into the public. If anyone else found out that I was in the habit of sleeping with the men who hired me to do private investigation.

If I was unlucky, I'd be branded one of those women who only pretended to be a PI and was actually doing a whole different sort of investigation.

"I'm sorry about the interruption to our work," Adam said stiffly. "But we're both consenting adults. I'm not sure you can give us any trouble for kissing in the hall."

Gray-haired Guy chuckled softly. "Well, I certainly can't judge you for wanting to kiss a beautiful woman, or do anything else. Time was, I would have tried the same thing. But doing it on company property is a whole different matter. I'm afraid we're going to have to write you both up, put it on your permanent record. And if it happens again, you'll both be terminated. Consider this fair warning."

I watched Adam draw himself up, furious at being spoken to like that—and, if I was guessing correctly, angry that I was being spoken about like I wasn't even here—and I almost stepped toward him and put a hand on his arm, just to get him to calm down. He was about to say something like that he owned the whole joint. I could see it. And if he did that, our cover was going to be blown and the case would be finished.

James, however, beat me to it. "Adam Miller!" he suddenly shouted, pointing at Adam. "That's who you are! I knew I recognized you! I've looked at your picture so many times, thinking how great it is that you did all of this when you were still so young, but with the beard and the glasses, I just didn't put two and two together." He paused, his eyes growing even bigger. "No wonder you're so good at sales!"

Adam cringed and made shushing motions with his hands, begging James to keep it down. "We're not here as ourselves," he said quickly. "So I'd appreciate it if you kept it down."

Jan and the exec both looked shocked and confused about all of this—and, no doubt, horrified that they'd just tried to write the CEO of the company up for having sex in the closet with someone who now didn't appear to be an employee at all—and Adam motioned for everyone to come closer.

Then he explained everything. The missing money, the fact that it had come from this office, and the idea that we'd come to go undercover and figure out what was going on. He introduced me as the top PI in the nation, which was embarrassing, and told them that if they told anyone else who we were, it would blow our cover and put our reputations at risk.

Then he turned to the lawyer in the room. "I'll need NDAs for everyone in this room, stating that they won't reveal our identities or why we're here. Can you take care of that?"

"Yes, sir," the lawyer said quickly. He sat down at the desk, opened his laptop, and went right to work.

Then Adam turned to everyone else. "We have a guy here that we're looking into, though we don't know if it's going to amount to anything. With any luck, we'll be out of your hair soon."

Gray-haired Guy nodded. "That works fine. Just don't be sneaking into closets anymore. If anyone else catches you, it's going to be impossible to explain why we didn't fire you on the spot."

Adam and I looked at each other, a wordless conversation going between us, and we both nodded.

"We won't." Adam stood up and looked at each of them. "Please have those NDAs faxed to my office in New York. And I'm counting on you to be on my team on this one. This is one of our best offices, and I don't want to have to close it because there are numbers here that don't add up."

Everyone quickly agreed to keep their mouths shut, responding to his CEO personality, and we turned and left the room without an escort.

"That," I said on the way to the elevators, "was way too close. We can't be seen together at all from here on out. Not if we're going to maintain our cover."

It had been fun while it lasted. But from here on out, Adam and I were going to have to be partners from different floors. And I was already wondering if I should move to a different hotel, just to keep him from showing up at my door at all hours of the day.

CHAPTER 22

ADAM

ADAM: *Anything on that guy from the New York office yet?*

Katie: *Nothing under the name he gave your company. His other name, though...*

I gasped and clutched my phone harder, despite myself. What the hell was she talking about? Other name? We'd hired a guy who had multiple identities? In New York?

And Houston had hired a guy who had faked his own college transcripts.

I slapped my forehead with my palm, cursing all the gods of HR. If there even was such a thing. What the hell was going on with the HR department, though, when mistakes like this were getting through?

Also, what the hell was with the ellipses at the end of that last text? If she had more information, why wasn't she just sending it on?

A second later, an email came in, and I could see why she hadn't sent a text. I opened up the email, then opened the doc that was attached to it, and started reading.

"Oh my freakin' goodness," I muttered.

This guy wasn't just weird about taking extra vacation time. He had an expunged record. Like... meaning that he'd gone to prison, or at least juvenile hall, and had then had those records bleached. Either he'd gone to juvie and had his record cleaned when he turned 18, or he had some really, really good contacts that were high up enough to clean up his record for him.

What. The. Hell.

Instead of texting again, I just dialed Katie's number. I wasn't happy about it. I wanted to rush right to her room, get in and sit down on her couch, and start asking questions. But since that situation in the execs' office, we'd been incredibly careful about being seen together. Come to think of it, I hadn't even seen her in the last couple of days. Not in the foyer of the building, not in the reception area of the hotel, not even in the dining room.

What was she doing, ordering nothing but room service and staying in her room until she knew I was out of the building?

And if she was, how did she know when I was out of the building?

She answered her phone at that moment, cutting off that useless train of thought.

"You got the email?" she asked without preamble.

"I did. What does this mean?"

She paused, probably to bite her lip or run her fingers along her chin the way she did when she was thinking, and when she spoke, her voice was deadly serious. "It means that he probably has some friends in very high places to be able to pull this off. It means that he applied to your company with a fake name and ID—probably things he created when he realized that even an expunged record is still attached to your name, in one way or another."

"What does that mean?" I asked again.

Hey, don't look at me that way. I wasn't used to dealing with the underworld or people with prison records. Katie was, and she was an expert, so as long as I had her, I was going to use her to learn everything I needed.

"It means that there would still be an asterisk attached to his name, that led to a file that didn't have anything in it," she explained. "But even if that file doesn't have anything in it, so the employer or whoever it is can't see what the person might have done, the file still exists."

"So the employer or whoever knows that they did something," I continued. "Well, that's a trap."

"Trap or safety mechanism?" she asked sharply. "If someone's had a record at any point, wouldn't you want to know about it? Even if you couldn't see what they'd done?"

Good point. "So why didn't my HR department find it?" I asked. "At this point I feel like we have to do a huge overhaul of how my company handles HR. We have a criminal up in New York and a guy who faked his transcripts down here."

"And two suspects," she replied. "Though I'm leaning more and more toward the guy in New York. I've just managed to unseal the records that they expunged."

"Oh, obviously," I said. "Because why would sealing records mean anything?"

"I'm good at my job," she said pointedly. "Which is why you hired me."

I cringed at that—both at the tone and at the not-so-subtle reminder that she was still working for me, despite the fact that we'd slept together several times.

And that thought reminded me of how it had felt to slide into her, my gaze taking her in as I pulled her onto my cock.

And that thought was pretty much totally unhelpful right now. Yeah, it was a good one, but it wasn't going to help us solve the problems in the company. I put it away for use later, when I was more at leisure, and jumped to my next question.

"So what did he do?"

"White-collar crime," she said immediately. "Stealing from stockbrokers he worked for."

I hit my forehead with my palm once again. "My goodness, my HR department needs a complete overhaul. They hired a guy who did exactly what we're looking for."

"Not intentionally," she noted. "He didn't give them the name that this record is attached to. So not only has he been stealing, but he's also guilty of identity theft. He must have an entirely new identity, complete with Social Security number and everything."

"Even more reason to fire him," I said quickly. "I say we head back to New York."

"The theft is coming from Houston," she reminded me. "We're in the right spot. The problem is, we're running out of time."

I groaned, my mind taking that jump right after her. She was right about that part. The finance department in New York had been very clear that the missing money was on the Houston accounts, not the New York accounts. So we were definitely in the right place.

As for the running out of time...

"How long do you think it'll be before someone leaks?" I asked quietly.

She didn't have to ask what I was talking about. We both knew that too many people already knew about our secret. The moment one of them got antsy, they'd tell someone else, and that someone else would tell someone else, and before you knew it, the entire office would know exactly who I was—and probably Katie as well—and our cover would be blown.

Whoever was stealing from the company would either get a whole lot better at hiding it or leave the company entirely, never to be seen again.

And they knew how our financial accounts looked and where the weaknesses were. Once they were out of the company, we would lose any ability to track them or stop them. We'd have to change everything about how we ran the spending accounts, just to protect ourselves.

"I'm surprised we haven't already heard about someone leaking," she said, answering the question I'd asked. "We both know that NDAs are great, but are only quasi-enforceable. And there are so many people they might tell by accident. Their wives or husbands. Their best friends. The guys they play basketball with, or the moms of their kids' best friends. They might not even think about it and blurt it out without remembering that they're sworn to secrecy."

"And once they do, our mission is over with," I finished for her.

"Exactly. In my experience, once your cover is blown, there's nothing to be done about it. The person responsible will run, and we'll be unmasked. Literally. If you want to continue the investigation, you'll have to find someone new to do it. And you won't be able to be personally involved anymore."

"So what do we do? In your professional opinion?"

I didn't usually take advice from other people. But I'd hired Katie to do a job, and I knew she was the best there was. If she told me one thing or another was the best option, I'd believe her.

"We keep working our angles here in Houston until we find something that fits," she said. "And we hope like hell no one unmasks us before we figure out who's stealing from your company."

I pressed my lips together, hating that answer and all the ways it could go wrong. But that was evidently all she had for me, because she followed it up with the idea that she needed to get some sleep and that she'd let me know if anything else came up.

Then she hung up like this had just been a business call and nothing more.

I hung up as well, my heart hammering at the idea that it had been a whole lot more than just business—and then hammering even harder at the thought that I needed to stop thinking of her that way. The sooner we got this case settled, the better.

Even if it meant I might never see her again.

⸻ ◉ ⸻

AN HOUR LATER, AFTER pacing the confines of my room again and again, until I was surprised I hadn't actually worn a groove in the carpet, I thought I had some ideas.

Walking had always helped me think, and it was especially useful when there was a problem to be solved. So I'd started pacing the moment I got off the phone with Katie. I knew there had to be a way through this. I knew there had to be something that we were missing.

There had to be a way to outsmart the gossip chain, get what we needed in Houston, and get out before it was too late to do our jobs.

The fact that I, who had started a company right out of college and grown it to one of the largest companies in the nation, couldn't see the freaking path forward was really, really starting to annoy me. I'd always been able to see the path forward. Hell, I'd been able to see things that no one else could see—although a lot of people had called me stupid at the time for thinking those things were possible.

They'd been wrong. And I'd known they were. Because I always knew what to do.

"Dammit," I muttered, swinging around and pacing back the other way, my strides long and forceful. I could feel a sheen of sweat starting to build on my skin, and I knew my hair was sticking straight out, courtesy of me constantly running my fingers through it.

I didn't care. I needed my brain to start giving me answers, and I needed it now.

I knew we had to stay in Houston. And I was starting to think that the best step was to actually ask the supervisors if they'd noticed anything strange. Surely now that they knew we were here and looking into a numbers issue, they'd have ideas. Most of them probably already had people in their departments that they kept a close eye on, and some idea of who might be the culprit.

"If you had to guess someone in your department was stealing from the company, who would it be?" I asked no one in particular. Because there was no one else in my room.

And in that moment, I realized what a very large part of the problem was. There was no one in the room. I always did my best brainstorming with a partner—someone to bounce ideas off of—and here I was alone, pacing in a hotel room like I was training for some sort of marathon.

I needed a partner. I needed the partner that I'd come to Houston with. Things had gone completely sideways since the last time I saw her, and it suddenly felt like things might have gone sideways because we'd stopped having our brainstorming sessions.

Maybe everything would become clear if we just got into the same room again.

I didn't stop to think any further than that. I definitely didn't think about whether it was a good idea to head to her room or not, given our new rules about not seeing each other.

I needed her with me if we were going to figure this thing out. So I took my sweat-sheened skin and my sweatsuit-clad body and headed right out my door, already turning for the elevator bank and the route to Katie's room.

We'd get this sorted out. I knew we would. And we'd probably come in under the deadline and under budget, too.

⸺ ◉ ⸺

SHE OPENED THE DOOR immediately, which made me realize that she definitely hadn't been sleeping, as I'd halfway feared she was.

She was also wearing pajamas.

And I'm not just talking about any old pajamas. These weren't some ratty cotton pants and a big T-shirt. These were silk. Or satin, maybe; I'd never really figured out what the difference was. The shorts barely covered her ass, and the top was incredibly tight.

Probably something she only put on right before she was getting into bed, I thought. Probably not something anyone else ever got to see.

So why on earth was she answering the door wearing it?

"I'm sorry, were you in bed?" I asked quickly.

145

"Getting ready for it," she said. "And you know you're not supposed to be up here. What if someone sees you? What if someone finds out you've been to my room in the middle of the night? We're not supposed to be seeing each other, Adam."

For a long, tense moment, I could only think of one thing. I didn't care if anyone saw us. Because standing here in front of her, with her dressed in an outfit so tiny that I could see every curve through it, made me think of nothing more than wanting to have her under my hands again. I wanted to walk right into her room, push her back onto that table behind her, spread her legs, and bury myself between them.

I wanted it so badly that I could already feel my cock starting to throb at the thought.

I pulled my thoughts back, though, trying desperately to remember why I'd actually come up here, and finally settled on it.

"I think better when I have someone to talk to," I said. And then I did walk into the room—though I walked right past her and toward the couch without touching her.

Hey, I do have some self-discipline.

"Let's put together a plan," I said quickly. "We don't have a lot of time to fool around on this one."

She walked after me, yanked my arm to turn me around, and got behind me, pushing me back toward the door. "And we can't afford to be caught together again, either, or we're out of the office entirely," she said firmly. She leaned forward, opened the door, and shoved me back out of it again. "The plan is this: I'm going to talk to Charles Ray one more time tomorrow. See if I can get anything from him. If I don't, and if he can clear himself, then we start working on new leads. And in the meantime, we don't tempt fate by hanging out in the same room. In the middle of the night. Got it?"

She looked at me expectantly, waiting for an answer, and I finally just nodded.

"Got it," I said. "Let me know how it goes."

"You'll be my first phone call," she assured me.

Then she closed the door in my face.

I turned and headed for my room, trying to remember if I'd brought any sleeping pills with me. Trying to figure out, beyond that, if I could order them from room service, or if the drugstore downstairs might have them. I doubted I'd brought anything like that with me, but I was definitely going to need something. Because between the issues at the office and the mental image of Katie in her lingerie, I didn't think I was going to get any sleep tonight without some help.

CHAPTER 23

I WOKE UP EARLY ENOUGH the next day that I thought I could probably get to the office before Adam had even started moving around. It wasn't that I didn't want to see him—I did—or that I didn't miss taking cabs with him to the office—I did—but that I knew we absolutely couldn't afford to be caught together again. The head of the office had told us quite clearly that if we were found together again, we'd be fired.

We'd already drawn far too much attention to ourselves with that first stunt, and I assumed it was only a matter of time until someone who had been in on that meeting spilled the beans about who we were—I was betting on James Andrews, myself, as he was evidently a big fan of Adam's. We needed to figure out who we were looking for before that happened.

If we didn't, there was a chance that all of our hard work, all the time we'd put into this office, would be a waste. And though yeah, I was going to get paid regardless, I really didn't want to let this case go without making a solid effort at closing it.

You might even say I was personally committed, at this point.

All of which led to me getting up at the break of dawn, more or less, suffering through the indignity of a shower at that time of the morning, dressing quickly, and hustling out of the hotel with one eye on the taxi ahead of me and one on the reception behind me.

I didn't see Adam. And I counted that as my mission accomplished. At least for this morning.

DURING THE RIDE TO the office, I went over my next mission. It started with a plan to get Charles Ray into my own—small—office, or maybe even into a larger room where we wouldn't have to sit right on top of each other to have a meeting. I didn't think Charles was the one who was stealing the money. I'd been through his expense account several times, and I could only find him putting money back into the system by evidently paying part of a vendor's bill on his own, rather than through the company accounts.

And though that would have made sense, if he was doing it to pay back the money he'd stolen, he wasn't paying back nearly enough to make up for $3 million.

I couldn't find him padding his accounts enough to steal that much, but I might be missing something. And I wouldn't know until I met with him and forced him to tell me the truth. Honestly, a very large part of me was hoping that he was the guy, just because it would mean we could close the case.

As the taxi pulled into the driveway of the office, I went through the plan I had to get that truth out of him. It wasn't sophisticated, but I was counting on him to fall for it, anyhow. I sure hoped he did.

Because my instincts—which were almost never off when it came to a case—were screaming at me that we didn't have much more time at this office before we blew our cover.

⸻ ❧ ⸻

"UM, YOU WANTED TO SEE me?" a voice said from the doorway of the conference room I'd scheduled for this meeting.

I looked up and saw Charles Ray there, looking both awkward and extremely nervous. And no wonder, I thought. It probably wasn't a good feeling to be called up to the finance department and told you had to have a meeting with one of the new accountants.

I was actually surprised that he'd come at all. I'd had a bet with myself that he would turn tail and run.

"Charles," I said, standing up and pasting a friendly smile onto my face. "Yes, thanks so much for coming up. Please, have a seat."

"Am I in trouble or something?" he asked, trying to make a joke of it.

I chuckled, but didn't put too much effort into it. After all, he was. And I didn't have the heart to lie to him about that.

"Nothing that we can't fix," I said, figuring that was close enough to the truth, and would hopefully put him at ease. Because I needed him to be cooperative.

I needed him to tell me exactly what he'd been doing with that spending account of his.

Once he was seated, I tidied the papers in front of me—which were totally unnecessary, as I knew exactly what I was going to say—and looked up at him, still trying to keep my face friendly. "Charles," I started, "The first thing I do whenever I come into any new department is to run a check on all the accounts I'm being put in charge of. I do a profit and loss, more or less, and a sort of unofficial audit of everyone. That includes going into personnel files, to get to know whoever I'm supposed to be tracking."

His face blanched at that part, and I gave myself a mental high-five. I wasn't sure which of those things had affected him, but something certainly had. And that boded very well for me coming out of this meeting with the truth about who he was and what he was doing.

"So when I was looking at your files, I saw some things come up that made me sort of curious," I continued.

"Like what?" he asked, his voice hoarse with nerves.

"Like the fact that your college transcripts are faked," I said bluntly. "I saw it when I was looking through your files, and when I printed them out, I knew I was right. Then I called the college to confirm. They've never even heard of you, Charles."

He opened his mouth and closed it again, then repeated the gesture, like he was a fish dying for a drink of water.

I just watched him, my face neutral. I wasn't going to help him out of this jam. I wanted to see how he handled it, because that was going to dictate how I handled the next question.

He closed his mouth and stared at me for a long moment, and I wondered whether he was trying to figure out whether he could make up a story or not. Whether I would believe him if he lied.

In the end, he must have realized that I already knew enough to know if he tried to lie to me about it.

"It's not my fault," he finally said in a rush. "Or rather... Well, I mean it is, obviously it is, because I was the one who did it. I was the one who didn't go to the school I was supposed to go to, and I was the one who made those fake transcripts. So I guess it was my fault. But it also wasn't. The thing is, my dad got really sick right when I was supposed to go to college, and suddenly there wasn't any money anymore. I mean, *no* money. Not even enough for them to pay their mortgage, and certainly not enough for them to pay the medical bills. I knew I couldn't spend any money to go to school, not with them in that situation, but I also knew that I needed that degree to get a good job. So I could help my mom take care of my dad."

His voice broke at that, and I glanced down at my notes. According to his personnel file, he'd recently taken time off for a death in the family.

"Your dad didn't make it, did he?" I asked gently, feeling rotten right down to the baby toe at having brought this out of him.

He just shook his head slowly and looked down, biting his lip. "It wasn't enough," he said. "No matter what treatments they tried, it was no use. He just kept getting sicker and sicker. And then one day, he finally gave up."

Oh shit. I'd hated the idea of forcing this guy to come clean, but now that I was hearing this sob story, I felt even worse.

"My dad was sick when I was young," I told him, leaning forward to take his hand. "I know how hard it can be to watch your parent going through that."

He looked back up at me and met my gaze. "Did your dad die?"

"He made it," I said, feeling guilty at having to give him that news, too. "But it was touch and go there for a while. It's awful to feel so helpless."

He took a deep breath and blew it out slowly. "I knew I couldn't tell anyone about my transcripts. I needed the money too badly. My parents needed the money. I guess I was sort of hoping no one would notice."

"It's your bad luck that I did," I said, drawing back.

And now for the really important part. Now that he was prepped and primed to tell me the truth, thinking I was his friend, I could ask what I really wanted to know. I looked up and met the gaze of my supervisor, who had appeared at the door. She had James with her, though he couldn't know what it was about. But I needed both of them to hear what Charles was telling me.

"So we know your transcripts are faked," I said, keeping my eyes on Jan's. "What about the problem with the numbers in your spending account?"

I hadn't thought he could go any paler, but he somehow did.

Still, it seemed that he'd decided to come clean about everything, because he started talking immediately.

"That's my fault, too," he said quickly. "I was putting the numbers in wrong when I ordered from specific distributors. Stupid, stupid mistake, but it wasn't intentional. Meant the vendors were getting paid more than they should have been, though, and once one of them was honest enough to tell me, I started putting the money back into the company's accounts on my own. I couldn't ask the vendors for refunds when it had been my fault to overpay them. But I started putting only half of their charges into the system, and paying the other half myself. I... I almost have it paid off already," he finished nervously. "I would have told someone, but I didn't think it was worth it. I figured I could get it taken care of and it wouldn't hurt anyone."

Wait. I frowned and looked down at the papers on the table in front of me, my eyes scanning through the numbers there.

What he said matched the notes exactly. I'd already known about it.

But could that really be *all* he'd done? He'd just described a con that would have been incredibly easy to pull off. Overpay the vendors you have a deal with, then go to their places of business and collect the balance in cash. Easy. Relatively clean. Almost untraceable.

But he'd been paying back the money. I'd known that, too.

But I'd been hoping there was more, I realized suddenly. I hadn't thought he was our guy, but I'd been hoping he was. And hearing him come clean so quickly about one problem made me realize that he definitely wasn't stealing millions of dollars.

He didn't have the constitution for it. Hell, he'd barely gotten away with faking his transcripts. He'd felt so guilty about it that I was betting he would have told someone within the next year, even without my probing.

If he was stealing millions of dollars, there was no way he'd be able to sit there and lie to my face.

Dammit.

Definitely not our guy, then.

"Sounds like you're working that one out on your own, then," I said, giving him a slight grin. "I don't blame you. You're right; getting the finance department involved would have made it a much bigger mess than it had to be. Still..."

I looked up at Jan and James, handing the reins over to them. I'd done my job. Now it was their turn.

"Still," James said, walking into the room, "the transcripts thing is a problem. You're really good at your job, and I don't want to fire you, but I'm going to have to write you up, and you're going to have to go on probation. I'll give you ninety days. Prove you can be trusted during that time, and we'll go back to normal employment. Do anything else fishy and that's the end. Understand?"

Charles nodded, his eyes big and wet at the possibility of being fired, and I gave another mental sigh.

I'd thought my instincts were always right when it came to a case like this. But I should have known right away that this wasn't our guy. He didn't have the backbone to pull off a con like the one we were looking at. Hell, I bet he didn't even steal creamer from the break room.

I should have seen it right away. And I would have, if I hadn't been so distracted by the man who'd hired me.

⎯⎯⎯◉⎯⎯⎯

"IT'S NOT CHARLES RAY," I muttered into my phone as I walked through the lobby and toward the street.

I wanted to get out of the building. I wanted to have some time to myself. And I wanted to make sure I didn't run into Adam now, when I was feeling sort of downtrodden and glum.

"Dammit," Adam muttered back, keeping his voice low.

He must still be in his cube, I thought. He didn't want anyone else to hear him.

"How do you know for sure?" he asked.

"I just did an interview with him where he basically told me his entire life story. And stealing from the company wasn't part of the narrative."

I heard him sigh, but he didn't argue with me. "Got it. So Houston's a bust, then. The one suspect we have turns out to be not a suspect, after all."

"Not a bust," I corrected. "We've got foundations here, now, and aliases that we can use moving forward. This particular suspect is a bust. But there will be others. We just have to keep our heads down and find them. Somewhere in the office, someone is stealing money from you. And I'm going to find them."

There was a grin in his voice when he answered. "You so sure of that?"

I felt an answering grin growing on my face. "I'm not going to rest until I find them. I've got a personal stake in this now. In case you hadn't noticed."

153

He chuckled. "A personal stake, eh? Why would that be?"

I leaned up against the side of the building, letting myself consider that question. I wouldn't have said I had a personal stake in the case if I was just getting paid to do a job.

When I thought about Adam, though, I felt a hot flash travel down my spine and right into my core. It wasn't love, I didn't think. I would never have called it something that serious. But it was definitely more than just a casual working relationship.

It was enough to make me want to see the case finished just so I could put a smile on his face.

"I like the guy who hired me," I answered, keeping it straight and simple.

"I'm thinking he kind of likes you, too," he said, his voice warm with meaning. "So what do we do now?"

"Start over again," I said with a sigh. "Back at the beginning. And this time, we work harder and faster, and we don't get caught in positions that might blow our cover."

CHAPTER 24

ADAM

THIS TIME WE WORK HARDER and faster, and we don't get caught in positions that might blow our cover.

It had made sense when she said it. So much sense that I'd agreed without even thinking about it. And I was pretty sure that she'd meant every single syllable of that. And that she meant starting immediately.

Which probably made me going to her room with a tray completely packed with breakfast foods a bad idea. Or... well, not a bad idea, since I was pretty freaking excited about it, but at least an idea that she was most definitely going to argue with me about.

But I'd thought about it during the hour when I was awake in the middle of the night, and I'd decided that before we started back at the beginning, we deserved a break from that case. And a break meant that we could actually see each other. Besides, it was Saturday, and no one from work was going to be hanging around at the hotel. They were all at home, probably still asleep, or at least doing something that had absolutely zero to do with Miller and Co.

They were almost definitely not thinking about what the two newest employees were doing. The only people who even knew for sure that we might be doing anything were Jan, James, the executive (whose name I'd never gotten, though I probably should have known him), and the corporate lawyer who had been in attendance.

I hoped they weren't thinking about what we might be doing, either. Because if they were, that was pretty creepy.

I got off the elevator with my cart in hand, turned right, and made my way toward Katie's door, actually having to stop myself from whistling a happy little tune.

Because on the list of ideas I'd had in my life, this one was pretty close to the top. I didn't think I'd ever surprised a woman with breakfast before, mostly because women didn't usually see me during this hour, but I couldn't think of anyone I'd rather surprise with food than Katie.

Besides, she'd been working really hard on this case, and had definitely gone above and beyond when it came to Charles Ray. He might have turned out to be the wrong guy, but she'd figured out his entire history in record time. Plus showed HR some holes in their systems. Plus identified several holes in the spending accounts we used. And the Houston office's security protocols.

I mean she'd done a whole lot more than just PI work over the last couple of weeks.

And beyond all that, she'd worked her way right into my brain. I wasn't positive whether it was anything more than that, and I was really dragging my feet about putting a label on it, particularly since I didn't know if I was ever going to see her again after we closed this case.

But the fact was, getting to see her lit up my entire world. I'd never had anything like that before, and I wasn't in a hurry to get rid of it.

Or her.

Anyhow, the You've Been Working So Hard thing was my official excuse for being up here. And I was going to use it to within an inch of my life if I had to.

Officially speaking, this was a celebratory breakfast. And I was sticking to that idea when she started arguing with me about how there wasn't anything to celebrate yet, and how we really couldn't afford to be seen together.

See? I already knew her well enough to know exactly what she was going to say.

I stopped outside her door, still grinning to myself, and looked over the tray. I'd ordered pretty much everything, on the off chance that she might like it, and the food was still piping hot. I could already feel myself starting to salivate at the idea of breakfast.

And the idea of having it with her.

I reached out and knocked on the door before I could follow that thought any further, and then waited the fifteen years it took for her to open the door. She took so long, in fact, that I was starting to wonder if she was still asleep.

I hadn't taken her for a late sleeper. But the moment the thought occurred to me, I started cussing at myself. Because she might be, and I just wouldn't know about it. And if she was, then this whole surprise was going to go to waste.

Then the door swung open and revealed a very tousled and insanely gorgeous Katie, in those same pajamas I'd admired the other night and looking like she'd just rolled out of bed. Her hair was wild with tangles, and her face was completely bare.

I didn't think I'd ever seen anything so beautiful in my life.

"You," I said, "are way too beautiful in the morning."

"You," she responded, "are a liar and a half. Also, what the hell are you doing at my room? I thought we agreed we weren't going to put ourselves in a position to get caught."

She didn't look nervous, though, and she didn't look mad. She looked... sleepy and beautiful and like she was happy to see me, though her mouth might say otherwise. In fact, she was so tousled and sexy and irresistible that...

I pushed the cart to the side, stepped through the door, and took her into my arms, needing to feel her up against me. I wanted her warmth and her scent and her presence all around me.

I wanted to make love to her in a room rather than a closet or a car. I wanted to make her mine. For reals, this time.

And when I took her in my arms, she didn't fight me. Instead, she melted into me, her face turning up to me and her eyes smiling as she bit her lips.

"What's all this?" she asked softly.

"I'm tired of trying to resist you," I told her truthfully.

"All that food is going to get cold," she said gently, teasing, her lips curling up into a sly sort of smile.

I leaned down and kissed her gently, my lips brushing over hers in a movement that was almost as teasing as her tone had been, and felt the goosebumps rising on her skin at the action.

When I pulled back, I was wearing a smile, too.

"That's the magic of room service," I said. "You can always reorder the food that might have gone cold."

She huffed out a breathy laugh, more sigh than giggle, and that was all the invitation I needed. I pulled her to me, slipped my arm down under her knees, and picked her up, cradling her to my chest like a precious treasure, her still sleep-warmed limbs loose and delicious in my arms.

And then I walked with her right to the bedroom. Because I was serious about the room and the bed and all of it this time. I'd taken this woman in a closet and in a car, and though both had been mind-glowingly wonderful experiences, I wanted something more.

I wanted to make love to her in a place that allowed us to go slow. To watch each other as we joined together. Maybe even to fall asleep afterward, in horizontal positions.

I laid her down on the bed, taking a moment to appreciate the fact that this was where she'd been sleeping when I showed up. The sheets were still warm from her, and I ran my hand over them, then moved to skim my fingers over the skin of her leg.

She arched up off the bed, gasping, and I felt my cock respond.

Damn you, I hissed inside my head at my cock. I'd meant to go slowly with her this time, but it was going to be very difficult if she kept doing things like that. My cock listened to her, not me.

Instead of reaching for her immediately, I stripped myself of my shirt and jeans, my actions growing faster and more frantic with every piece of clothing. The brush of the cloth against my skin had made me realize that I couldn't be slow this time. I had Katie in bed in seconds, spread out among the blankets and sheets, and she was warm and pliant and ready.

I could see her arching up off the bed, her eyes hooded and her lips parted, and I didn't have to ask to know she was wet and ready for me.

She wanted me as badly as I wanted her. And this time, we weren't going to hide it.

When I pulled my jeans off, her eyes went immediately to my cock, darkening with pleasure and need before they came back up to me.

"Are you just going to stand there, or are you going to come to bed?" she whispered.

I went to bed. I crawled over her and settled between her legs, my lips going to hers and my hands grasping one wrist and pulling it above her head to hold her still. I kissed her deep and hard, my tongue roving into her mouth with absolute ownership, and she opened up underneath me. Ready. Wanting.

Hot and beautiful and mine. At least for the moment.

I reached down and pulled the shorts of her pajamas to the side, finding her wet center and running my fingers through the damp heat there, and she jerked and gasped underneath me. She jerked even harder when I pushed one finger into her, moving it in and out in a slow, pulsing movement that had her writhing on the bed within moments. She tried to bring her legs up, to take my finger deeper, but I pinned them to the bed, watching her struggle against me.

"Fuck," she said, breathing heavily. "Please. Adam, please. Stop teasing."

I leaned in and brushed my lips against her neck. "What do you want?"

She threw her head back, giving me better access to her neck. "You," she gasped. "Please."

As much as I wanted to keep teasing her, I knew I didn't have it in me. My cock was already aching with the need to have her, my skin feverish with wanting. I was burning up from the inside, and she was the only cure.

And damn, did I want that cure. I wanted it again and again, until I couldn't keep my eyes open anymore.

I settled down between her legs, drew her shorts further to the side, and pushed into her, watching her face as I slid my cock up to the base, then drew it back out again.

Her mouth opened in a silent scream and she bucked against me, begging me with her body for more. Her legs moved up to wrap around my hips, her hands going into my hair, and she opened her eyes and stared right at me.

"Harder," she demanded. "Please."

This was the woman I felt like I'd been waiting for my entire life. Smart, sexy, and incredibly demanding.

And so I gave her exactly what she wanted.

⸺ ◉ ⸺

LATER, WHEN I FINALLY got out of bed and started thinking about the rest of the world again, my first thought was of my email. Yes, I know. It sounds odd. But Oliver had promised to send me more information on the guy we'd been watching in New York, and HR's files on him, and I wanted to see if he'd sent along the information yet.

After all, the one lead we'd had here in Houston was dead. And though I might have just spent the entire morning with Katie's body up against mine, her eyes on mine and her breath filling my soul, I

159

still needed to figure out what was going on with the accounting in
my company.

I needed to figure out who we were going to look at next. And
how we were going to do it. Katie had said we were going to have to
start at the bottom again and work our way back up to actually
having a suspect, and I agreed with her there.

But it sure would be nice if we could get a leg up from someone
Oliver already had suspicions about. Sure, I would have to figure out
how a person in New York was causing money to disappear from the
Houston office, but there were probably a hundred ways that could
be happening.

I opened the laptop I'd brought up to Katie's room with me and
quickly logged into my company email, my eyes going quickly
through the list in my inbox to look for the familiar names.

Which was when I saw something from Samuel Jennings.

Who the hell was Samuel Jennings, and why did that name sound
so familiar?

I clicked on the email, wondering, and saw when it came up that
Samuel Jennings was the exec who had been in on the meeting
where they'd told Katie and me that we'd been caught. Which made
sense, I supposed. He'd known to email me on my company account
because he knew who I was.

Though that didn't explain why he was emailing me.

I scanned through the email, reading quickly enough that I ended
up at the signature without a true idea of what the email was trying
to say. I went through it again, more slowly this time, and gasped.

"What is it?" Katie asked, coming up behind me. "You look like
you've either had really great news or really terrible news."

"I'm not sure yet," I said quietly. "Look."

I turned the laptop to her and let her read the email, watching her
face as she read it and knowing exactly what she was seeing. The
Houston office had hosted a meeting of the execs and the supervisors
from several different departments. Samuel had told them that he'd
noticed some inconsistencies in the numbers, and that he needed to
know what was going on. He'd been vague enough that no one
would ever guess that I was involved, or that he was working on
behalf of the New York office.

He'd just told them that there were numbers that didn't add up,
and that he thought something funny was going on.

He'd asked the supervisors for names and email addresses of employees that they were suspicious of. People who had been acting odd lately, or taking a lot of time off, or had recently made very large purchases.

And it had turned out that the supervisors had been paying attention, not only to their departments, but to the departments on other floors, as well. They'd handed him a list of names of people that deserved a closer look.

He'd taken one step further and looked into those names himself. And he'd come to the conclusion that many of the people had been turned in only because they had personal conflicts with the supervisors, or other employees in their departments. They weren't worth looking into, though he'd told his own assistant to keep an eye on the activity in those departments, to make sure everyone stayed focused on their work rather than any petty arguments.

Three of the men, though, had warranted his attention. They'd come in at the same time and had all had large gaps in their background checks. Nothing big enough to alert HR to a problem. But they had asterisks on their records, all the same.

Those three men were included in the body of the email. We had their names, their physical addresses, their Social Security numbers, and their email addresses.

Everything Katie would need to find out more about them.

And Samuel had ended with the advice to look at these men and find out what we could through alternative routes. Routes that might not be open to him.

If there's money missing in our office, he wrote, *I'm betting it's one of these men. I know your first suspect didn't work out. I would look at these ones next. Please let me know if there's anything else I can do to help.*

Katie finished the email and looked up at me, her face caught between surprise and victory. "So not from the very start, then," she said.

I knew exactly what she meant. We had to find out what these men had been up to and whether they were responsible for the missing money. We had to find a way to get to know them, and Katie was going to have to get into their records and start going through their information.

But we weren't starting from scratch this time, thanks to Samuel. And this time, we were going into it as partners, rather than two people who just happened to be working together.

THE END

Finance

BE THE PLAYER, NOT the piece...

Adam Miller is just your average billionaire CEO of one of the largest tech and marketing companies in the country.

Katie Walters is just the PI he hires to figure out how one of his employees is stealing money from the company accounts.

But when they agree to go undercover together in one of his satellite offices, they're signing a contract neither of them fully understands. Their first meeting is electric, and before long, they're fighting a mutual attraction that they both know is a bad idea. When that attraction gets the better of them, they find themselves facing two problems: 1. You don't have sex with your boss—or the woman you've hired as your PI, and 2. Their attraction toward each other might just mean the thief ends up getting away.

Undercover Boss Series

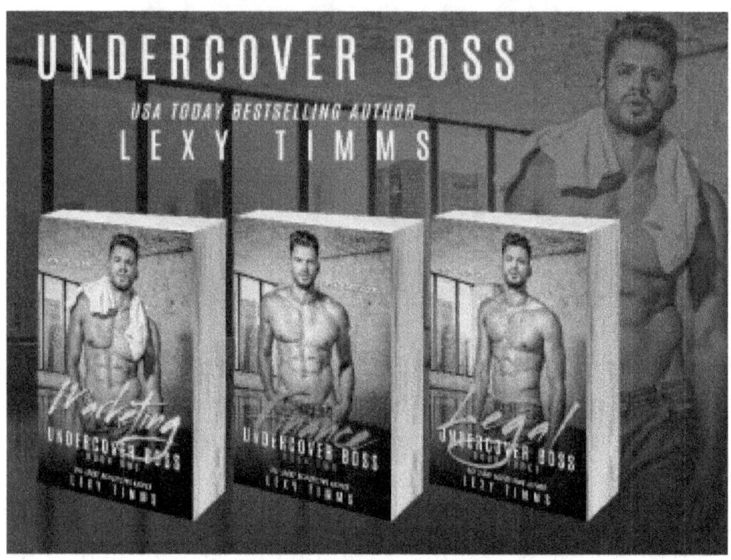

Book 1 – Marketing
Book 2 – Finance
Book 3 – Legal

Find Lexy Timms:

LEXY TIMMS NEWSLETTER:
http://eepurl.com/9i0vD
Lexy Timms Facebook Page:
https://www.facebook.com/SavingForever
Lexy Timms Website:
http://www.lexytimms.com

Want to read more...

For FREE?

Sign up for Lexy Timms' newsletter
And she'll send you updates on new releases, ARC copies of books
and a whole lotta fun!
Sign up for news and updates!
http://eepurl.com/9i0vD

More by Lexy Timms:

FROM BEST SELLING AUTHOR, Lexy Timms, comes a billionaire romance that'll make you swoon and fall in love all over again.

Jamie Connors has given up on men. Despite being smart, pretty, and just slightly overweight, she's a magnet for the kind of guys that don't stay around.

Her sister's wedding is at the foreground of the family's attention. Jamie would be fine with it if her sister wasn't pressuring her to lose weight so she'll fit in the maid of honor dress, her mother would get off her case and her ex-boyfriend wasn't about to become her brother-in-law.

Determined to step out on her own, she accepts a PA position from billionaire Alex Reid. The job includes an apartment on his property and gets her out of living in her parent's basement.

Jamie must balance her life and somehow figure out how to manage her billionaire boss, without falling in love with him.

** The Boss is book 1 in the Managing the Bosses series. All your questions won't be answered in the first book. It may end on a cliff hanger.

For mature audiences only. There are adult situations, but this is a love story, NOT erotica.

***EVIL* begins when you start to treat people as things...**

A KIDNAPPING ISN'T how I expected to meet the woman of my dreams.

But when my brother, intent on proving himself as the hardcore gangster he wants to be, comes up with the idea to kidnap the daughter of a powerful crime boss, I know I can't stop him. And that's how I meet Charlotte.

Beautiful, intelligent, graceful – and hurting from the life she's been trapped into living. She wants to get out of this world just as much as I do, and it doesn't take long till we fall for each other, hard and fast.

Except time is running out for both of us.

If we're going to be together, we need to act fast – and do something that we can never renege on...

Book 1 – Payment for Sin
Book 2 – Atonement Within
Book 3 – Declaration of Love

THE ONE YOU CAN'T FORGET

Emily Rose Dougherty is a good Catholic girl from mythical Walkerville, CT. She had somehow managed to get herself into a heap trouble with the law, all because an ex-boyfriend has decided to make things difficult.

Luke "Spade" Wade owns a Motorcycle repair shop and is the Road Captain for Hades' Spawn MC. He's shocked when he reads in the paper that his old high school flame has been arrested. She's always been the one he couldn't forget.

Will destiny let them find each other again? Or what happens in the past, best left for the history books?

*** This is book 1 of the Hades' Spawn MC Series. All your questions may not be answered in the first book.*

FORTUNE RIDERS MC
BILLIONAIRE BIKER
LEXY TIMMS
Download For
FREE
Lexy
Timms

THE
DEAD OF NIGHT
SERIES
USA TODAY BESTSELLING AUTHOR
LEXY TIMMS
Abduction
Bribery
Corruption

THE
HEAT OF NIGHT
SERIES
USA TODAY BESTSELLING AUTHOR
LEXY TIMMS
Depravity
Scandal
Disgrace

Don't miss out!

Click the button below and you can sign up to receive emails whenever Lexy Timms publishes a new book. There's no charge and no obligation.

Did you love *Marketing*? Then you should read *Taken By The Mob Boss* by Lexy Timms!

EVIL begins when you start to treat people as things…

A kidnapping isn't how I expected to meet the woman of my dreams.

But when my brother, intent on proving himself as the hardcore gangster he wants to be, comes up with the idea to kidnap the daughter of a powerful crime boss, I know I can't stop him. And that's how I meet Charlotte.

Beautiful, intelligent, graceful – and hurting from the life she's been trapped into living. She wants to get out of this world just as much as I do, and it doesn't take long till we fall for each other, hard and fast.

Except time is running out for both of us.

If we're going to be together, we need to act fast – and do something that we can never renege on...

A DARK MAFIA ROMANCE SERIES
Book 1 – Taken By The Mob Boss
Book 2 – Truce With The Mob Boss
Book 3 – Taking Over The Mob Boss
Book 4 – Trouble For The Mob Boss
Book 5 – Tailored By The Mob Boss
Book 6 – Tricking By The Mob Boss
Read   more   at   Lexy   Timms's   site.

Also by Lexy Timms

A Bad Boy Bullied Romance
I Hate You
I Hate You A Little Bit
I Hate You A Little Bit More

A Burning Love Series
Spark of Passion
Flame of Desire
Blaze of Ecstasy

A Chance at Forever Series
Forever Perfect
Forever Desired
Forever Together

A Dark Mafia Romance Series
Taken By The Mob Boss

A Dating App Series
I've Been Matched
You've Been Matched
We've Been Matched

A "Kind of" Billionaire
Taking a Risk
Safety in Numbers
Pretend You're Mine

A Maybe Series
Maybe I Should
Maybe I Shouldn't
Maybe I Did

Assisting the Boss Series

<u>Billion Reasons</u>
<u>Duke of Delegation</u>
<u>Late Night Meetings</u>
<u>Delegating Love</u>
<u>Suitors and Admirers</u>

BBW Romance Series
<u>Capturing Her Beauty</u>
<u>Pursuing Her Dreams</u>
<u>Tracing Her Curves</u>

Beating the Biker Series
<u>Making Her His</u>
<u>Making the Break</u>
<u>Making of Them</u>

Betrayal at the Bay Series
<u>Devil's Bay</u>
<u>Devil's Deceit</u>
<u>Devil's Duplicity</u> (Coming Soon)

Billionaire Banker Series
<u>Banking on Him</u>
<u>Price of Passion</u>
<u>Investing in Love</u>
<u>Knowing Your Worth</u>
<u>Treasured Forever</u>
<u>Banking on Christmas</u>
<u>Billionaire Banker Box Set Books #1-3</u>

Billionaire CEO Brothers
<u>Tempting the Player</u>
<u>Late Night Boardroom</u>
<u>Reviewing the Perfomance</u>
<u>Result of Passion</u>
<u>Directing the Next Move</u>
<u>Touching the Assets</u>

Billionaire Holiday Romance Series

<u>The Heart Needs</u>
<u>The Heart Wants</u>
<u>The Heart Knows</u>

Conquering Warrior Series
<u>Ruthless</u>

Counting the Billions
<u>Counting the Days</u>
<u>Counting On You</u>
<u>Counting the Kisses</u>

Cry Wolf Reverse Harem Series
<u>Beautiful & Wild</u>
<u>Misunderstood</u>
<u>Never Tamed</u>

Darkest Night Series
<u>Savage</u>
<u>Vicious</u>
<u>Brutal</u>
<u>Sinful</u>
<u>Fierce</u>

Diamond in the Rough Anthology
<u>Billionaire Rock</u>
<u>Billionaire Rock - part 2</u>

Dirty Little Taboo Series
<u>Flirting Touch</u>
<u>Denying Pleasure</u>
<u>Forbidding Desire</u>
<u>Craving Passion</u>

Dominating PA Series
<u>Her Personal Assistant - Part 1</u>
<u>Her Personal Assistant - Part 2</u>
<u>Her Personal Assistant Box Set</u>

Fake Billionaire Series

Faking It
Temporary CEO
Caught in the Act
Never Tell A Lie
Fake Christmas
Fake Billionaire Box Set #1-3

Firehouse Romance Series
Caught in Flames
Burning With Desire
Craving the Heat
Firehouse Romance Complete Collection

Forging Billions Series
Dirty Money
Petty Cash
Payment Required

For His Pleasure
Elizabeth
Georgia
Madison

Fortune Riders MC Series
Billionaire Biker
Billionaire Ransom
Billionaire Misery
Fortune Riders Box Set - Books #1-3

Fragile Series
Fragile Touch
Fragile Kiss
Fragile Love

Great Temptation Series
The Devil's Footsteps
Heaven's Command
Mortals Surrender

Hades' Spawn Motorcycle Club

<u>One You Can't Forget</u>
<u>One That Got Away</u>
<u>One That Came Back</u>
<u>One You Never Leave</u>
<u>One Christmas Night</u>
<u>Hades' Spawn MC Complete Series</u>

Hard Rocked Series
<u>Rhyme</u>
<u>Harmony</u>
<u>Lyrics</u>

Heart of Stone Series
<u>The Protector</u>
<u>The Guardian</u>
<u>The Warrior</u>

Heart of the Battle Series
<u>Celtic Viking</u>
<u>Celtic Rune</u>
<u>Celtic Mann</u>
<u>Heart of the Battle Series Box Set</u>

Heistdom Series
<u>Master Thief</u>
<u>Goldmine</u>
<u>Diamond Heist</u>
<u>Smile For Me</u>
<u>Your Move</u>
<u>Green With Envy</u>
<u>Saving Money</u>

Highlander Wolf Series
<u>Pack Run</u>
<u>Pack Land</u>
<u>Pack Rules</u>

Hollyweird Fae Series
<u>Inception of Gold</u>

Love You Series
Love Life
Need Love
My Love

Managing the Billionaire
Never Enough
Worth the Cost
Secret Admirers
Chasing Affection
Pressing Romance
Timeless Memories
Managing the Billionaire Box Set Books #1-3

Managing the Bosses Series
The Boss
The Boss Too
Who's the Boss Now
Love the Boss
I Do the Boss
Wife to the Boss
Employed by the Boss
Brother to the Boss
Senior Advisor to the Boss
Forever the Boss
Christmas With the Boss
Billionaire in Control
Billionaire Makes Millions
Billionaire at Work
Precious Little Thing
Priceless Love
Valentine Love
The Cost of Freedom
Trick or Treat
The Night Before Christmas
Gift for the Boss - Novella 3.5
Managing the Bosses Box Set #1-3
Managing the Bosses Novellas

Worth It Series
<u>Worth Billions</u>
<u>Worth Every Cent</u>
<u>Worth More Than Money</u>

You & Me - A Bad Boy Romance
<u>Just Me</u>
<u>Touch Me</u>
<u>Kiss Me</u>

Standalone
<u>Wash</u>
<u>Loving Charity</u>
<u>Summer Lovin'</u>
<u>Love & College</u>
<u>Billionaire Heart</u>
<u>First Love</u>
<u>Frisky and Fun Romance Box Collection</u>
<u>Beating Hades' Bikers</u>
<u>Everyone Loves a Bad Boy</u>

Watch for more at <u>Lexy Timms's site</u>.

About the Author

"Love should be something that lasts forever, not is lost forever." Visit USA TODAY BESTSELLING AUTHOR, LEXY TIMMS https://www.facebook.com/SavingForever *Please feel free to connect with me and share your comments. I love connecting with my readers.* Sign up for news and updates and freebies - I like spoiling my readers! http://eepurl.com/9i0vD website: www.lexytimms.com Dealing in Antique Jewelry and hanging out with her awesome hubby and three kids, Lexy Timms loves writing in her free time. MANAGING THE BOSSES is a bestselling 10-part series dipping into the lives of Alex Reid and Jamie Connors. Can a secretary really fall for her billionaire boss?

Read more at Lexy Timms's site.